WISH UPON A HORSE

Also by Maggie Dana

Keeping Secrets, Timber Ridge Riders (Book 1)
Racing into Trouble, Timber Ridge Riders (Book 2)
Riding for the Stars, Timber Ridge Riders (Book 3)
The Golden Horse of Willow Farm, Weekly Reader Books
Remember the Moonlight, Weekly Reader Books
Best Friends series, Troll Books

TIMBER RIDGE RIDERS
∾ Book Four ∾

WISH UPON A HORSE

Maggie Dana

PAGEWORKS PRESS

Wish Upon a Horse © 2013 Maggie Dana
www.maggiedana.com

This is a work of fiction. While references may be made to actual
places or events, all names, characters, incidents, and locations
are from the author's imagination and do not resemble any
actual living or dead persons, businesses, or events.
Any similarity is coincidental.

ISBN 978-0-9851504-3-3

Edited by Judith Cardanha
Cover by Margaret Sunter
Interior design by Anne Honeywood
Published by Pageworks Press
Text set in Sabon

in memory of
Whippoorwill Siskin
1972 – 2004

1

THE LAST THING KATE MCGREGOR EXPECTED was a letter from her father, but there it was, propped against the coffee pot when she got home from the barn. She glanced at the postmark—ten days from an outpost in the Amazon jungle to central Vermont. Not bad, considering the letter probably spent five of those ten days in a leather pouch covered with beads and feathers before it even reached civilization.

Kate ripped open the flimsy blue envelope and unfolded a single sheet of paper. It began, "Dear Katherine," which meant Dad was about to tell her something he thought she didn't want to hear. She scanned the brief letter, then read it again slowly, to make sure she understood.

He would be staying in Brazil longer than expected and had written to Liz Chapman to ask if Kate could remain with them until Thanksgiving, maybe even longer. He was sorry to disappoint her, but—

Kate let out a whoop.

"What's up?" Holly Chapman said. She walked into the kitchen and plunked her laptop on the table.

"This." Kate waved the letter. "It's from my dad."

Holly's blue eyes widened. "Why didn't he e-mail you?"

"Du-uhh," Kate said. "There's no Internet in the jungle." Her father had been in the Amazon since early June, identifying and cataloging rare butterflies. His last communication was a postcard three weeks ago that said he hoped to find a blue morphos with a wingspan of six inches.

"What did he say?" Holly said.

"He's written to your mom."

"Why?"

Kate's excitement bubbled over. "To ask if I can stay here through November."

"Like come to school with me and *everything*?" Holly said. She whipped off her baseball hat, then grabbed Kate's hands and whirled her in a circle.

"I guess," Kate said, feeling breathless.

It was almost too good to be true. Instead of going back to Connecticut, Kate would stay in Vermont and go to Holly's high school—for a few months, anyway. They would be freshmen this year, and despite Holly's warnings that the teachers were really tough, Kate didn't care. Anything, even sharing classes with their arch rival, Angela Dean, was better than her old school where everyone ignored her. Besides, she'd be going to school with Holly.

They'd been best friends ever since Kate had taken the summer job as Holly's companion when she was still confined to a wheelchair. So much had changed. Holly had learned to walk and to ride her horse again, Kate had worked in a movie, and they'd met a couple of really cute guys.

Holly gave a dramatic sigh. "So this means I'll have to put up with you till when, Thanksgiving?" She laid a hand on her brow. "I'm not sure I'll be able to stand it."

"No problem," Kate said, trying to keep a straight face. "I'll ask Angela if I can stay with her instead."

"Yeah, right." Holly opened her laptop. "I just found this," she said.

Liver chestnut gelding. Excellent bloodlines, no vices. Needs a little TLC. Will make a great event horse with the right trainer.

"TLC?" Kate said.

Holly grinned. "Trot, lope, canter?"

"Idiot," Kate said. "I think it means 'tender, loving care.'"

"In other words" Holly said, "the horse is a wreck." She clicked another link. "How about this one?"

Strawberry roan mare, sixteen hands, good jumper, owner going to college.

"I hate roans," Kate said. "Who wants to ride a pink horse?"

"Beggars can't be choosers," Holly said, flipping screens.

Kate flinched. All she had to spend on the horse of her dreams was the money she'd earned that summer working for Liz, Holly's mom, and riding as a stunt-double in the *Moonlight* film.

Three thousand dollars.

At first, it seemed like more than enough, and it was all hers, sitting in her brand new savings account, waiting for her to find just the right horse. She'd never dreamed of having so much money. But the moment she and Holly began to look at horse classifieds, Kate realized she was fooling herself. If she bought a horse for three thousand, there'd be nothing left over for its upkeep, the vet and the farrier bills, a saddle and a bridle, and all the other stuff she needed, which meant she could only afford to spend two thousand, maybe twenty-five hundred, on the horse itself.

"Here's a good one," Holly said.

Gray gelding, five years old, shown successfully in hunter classes last season.

She stopped and frowned. "Uh, oh. They're asking five thousand."

Kate sank into a chair and pulled off her muck boots. All the horses that sounded promising were wickedly expensive, and the ones she could afford were too young, too old, or too small.

"This one's *perfect*," Holly cried.

Bay mare, fabulous jumper, seven years old. Fifteen hundred dollars, or best offer.

"Wow," Kate said. She jumped up and leaned over Holly's shoulder. "Where? Show me."

Holly pointed to the bottom of the screen.

Kate's face fell. "You dummy," she said. "It's only thirteen hands."

"Whoops," Holly said. "I guess I missed that."

"I'll never find anything," Kate wailed.

"You can always share Magician," Holly said.

"I know, and thanks," Kate said.

But it wasn't the same as having her own horse. She adored Magician, Holly's black gelding. But now that Holly was back on her feet and riding him again, Kate had to beg and borrow rides whenever she could. For most of the summer, she'd been schooling Buccaneer, but he'd just been taken to his owner's farm out west. Kate missed him like mad. He loved peppermint Life Savers and loathed Angela Dean. Angela had ridden him, just once and jerked his mouth so hard he dumped her in a brush jump.

The garage door cranked open.

"Mom's home," Holly said. She flicked her blond ponytail and crammed her pink baseball cap back on. It had *Boss Mare* across the front and it matched her pink t-shirt that said, *Barn Brats Rule*. "Let's ask her where you can find a cheap horse."

"I already did," Kate said.

Liz Chapman ran the Timber Ridge riding stable. She was plugged into the local horse world and had promised to keep her ears and eyes open. She'd also warned Kate not to get her hopes up. Good horses, especially affordable ones, were hard to find.

"So we'll ask her again," Holly said.

But Liz shook her head. "I told you it wouldn't be easy," she said wearily, dumping two bags of groceries on the kitchen table.

"Mom," Holly said. "That's no help. Can't you think of *some* place we can look?" She bit into a Granny Smith apple, then pulled cereal and cans of soup from the bag and put them away.

"I'm sorry, kids. I've looked everywhere, but nothing's turned up." Liz handed Kate a bottle of detergent to stash beneath the sink. "If I had any extra cash, I'd help you out, but—"

"That's okay," Kate said. She knew Liz was struggling to make ends meet. Holly's medical treatments had been super expensive and insurance had only covered half of them. No way could Liz afford to loan Kate money toward a horse.

"So ask Angela," Holly muttered. "She's got tons of money."

"That reminds me," Liz said, tucking a hunk of blond hair behind one ear. "I ran into Mrs. Dean in the village. She's hired a new trainer for Angela, and—"

"But, Mom," Holly protested, "*you're* Angela's trainer. Why does she need another one?"

"I guess Mrs. Dean wants more than I can deliver," Liz said, with a shrug that didn't fool Kate for a minute.

Angela's mother ruled the Timber Ridge Homeowners' Association with an iron fist. Whatever Mrs. Dean wanted, she usually got, except when it came to the barn. She'd tried repeatedly to get Liz fired, but all her attempts had failed because Liz was good at her job—the riding team won ribbons and the kids adored her. Now it looked as if Mrs. Dean was doing an end run around Liz, and there was nothing she could do about it.

"What's his name?" Holly said.

"Vincent King."

Kate ran through her mental list of horse professionals. She knew them all from reading back issues of equine magazines, but this one didn't ring any bells. Maybe he was a newcomer or not famous enough to have his name in *Dressage Today* or *Chronicle of the Horse.*

"He'll be coaching Angela for the Labor Day show," Liz said, then added, "Mrs. Dean also told me that Angela's cousin is coming to stay with them."

"Why?" Holly said.

"Her parents are going to Japan for a year," Liz said. "Courtney didn't want to go with them, so—"

"—we're stuck with her," Holly said, making a face.

"Does she ride?" Kate said.

This would change the riding team dynamics. Another rider, with her own horse, would push Kate even further down the barn's totem pole. In fact, she'd fall off the bottom and end up as a groom—which was fine, as long as it was for Holly or one of the other riders Kate liked. She'd clean tack, run errands, and groom horses for Robin, Sue, and Jennifer until her arms wore out. But no way would she lift a brush for Princess Angela or her mysterious cousin.

Liz shrugged. "Mrs. Dean didn't say."

"Oh, Mom," Holly said, rolling her eyes. "You're hopeless."

Kate gave her a swift kick. "She's the best mom in the world."

"Thanks," Liz said, then patted the front of her khaki vest. "Now where did I put it?" From one over-stuffed pocket she pulled a broken spur, from another came a half-empty tube of wormer. "It's in here, some-where," she muttered, dumping barn keys and braiding elastics on the counter.

"What is?" Holly said.

"Aha," Liz said. She pulled out a crumpled envelope. "I had a letter from Kate's father today."

"And?" Holly said.

For a moment, Kate held her breath. Suppose Liz didn't want her to stay. It wasn't as if Holly needed her any more. If Liz said no, she'd have to go back to her aunt's cottage in the village. Aunt Marion was okay, but she knew nothing about kids and spent most of her time in the garden with her prize-winning roses.

"Of course, Kate can stay," Liz said. "That is, if she wants to."

"Are you sure?" Kate said, feeling shy. "I mean, I don't—"

Liz cut her off. "I know what you're trying to say, Kate, but you've no idea how much you mean to Holly and me. You're part of our family."

"You bet she is," Holly said. "We're more like sisters than ever, especially now Kate's a blonde."

Holly's words stung, even though she was teasing. The night before her screen test for the *Moonlight* film, Kate had bleached her mouse-brown hair, convinced it would give her a better chance of beating the dark-haired Angela for the stunt-double role. But the whole thing backfired when it turned out that the star of the movie— the glamorously blond Tess O'Donnell—would be wearing a dark wig and so would her double. Despite Angela's best efforts at sabotage, Kate won the role, and now she couldn't wait for her hateful hair to grow out.

Holly wrapped her arms around Kate. "But, honestly, Mom, Kate and I need to stick together, especially now that Angela's cousin is moving in. I bet she's a moron."

"With squinty eyes," Kate said.

"And fangs," Holly said, baring her teeth.

Liz sighed. "It's not fair to judge people before you meet them. You ought to know that by now."

Holly pretended to look repentant. So did Kate, but

they both knew the real deal. Angela on her own was bad enough. With a newly arrived cousin to help out, there'd be no end to the tricks she could pull to make Kate's life miserable.

* * *

Kate plumped up her bed pillows and settled down with the latest *Young Rider* magazine. Except she wasn't reading it, Holly noticed. Kate's eyes were focused elsewhere.

"What time is it?" Kate said.

Holly checked her watch. "Five minutes later than the last time you asked."

Kate had been in a panic ever since nine o'clock because Nathan hadn't called. Holly still found it hard to believe—her best friend hanging out with Nathan Crane, the movie star. He had the lead role in *Moonlight*, and Holly's boyfriend—well, her sort of boyfriend—Adam Randolph, had been Nathan's stunt-double for the riding scene with Kate.

That was something else Holly found hard to believe.

Adam had known Nathan since kindergarten but never thought to tell Holly and Kate that his best buddy had become a famous movie star.

Boys, Holly thought. *They just don't get it.*

The scene had been awesome—Adam riding Domino, and Kate in a gossamer white dress that streamed behind her as she galloped Magician to escape the zombies. It was all cameras, lights, and special effects, but it looked like fairytale magic to Holly. She'd relished every moment. It was exciting enough to make her want a career in film when she grew up. With horses, of course.

Kate's cell phone bleeped. She snatched it off her bedside table, shot Holly a huge grin, and leaped out of bed. Hugging the phone to her ear, she disappeared into the bathroom and shut the door. She'd probably be in there for an hour. Last night's phone call with Nathan had stretched until midnight.

Holly didn't envy Kate. She wouldn't get to see Nathan for ages. He lived in California, and next week he was off to Romania. They were shooting the rest of *Moonlight* in a castle with so many turrets and dungeons that Holly was convinced it had belonged to Dracula.

It would take another six months to finish the film, but the director had promised them tickets to the premiere in New York. Just her and Kate and Adam ... and Mom, of course. He hadn't invited Angela.

2

AFTER BARN CHORES THE NEXT MORNING, Kate and Holly saddled up and headed for the woods. Holly rode Magician, with Kate beside her on Rebel. The chestnut gelding snorted and danced sideways, pretending to be scared of a pile of rocks.

"Silly boy," Kate said, patting his neck.

He belonged to Jennifer West, the barn's newest rider. She'd asked Kate to exercise him while she was on vacation. Rebel loved to jump and Kate was sorely tempted by signs along the trail that pointed to the barn's cross-country course.

"You gonna try it?" Holly said.

Kate shook her head. "Better not," she said. "This is my first time on Rebel."

"Jennifer won't mind," Holly said. "You're the best rider in the barn, and Rebel jumps like a kangaroo."

But Kate didn't want to risk it. She'd gotten into trouble on the cross-country course before, jumping a horse without permission. Liz had grounded her for that one. "You mom would kill me."

"I wish she'd let me jump the course," Holly said.

"She will," Kate said. "Be patient."

Patience wasn't exactly Holly's strong suit. Before her accident two years ago, she'd been a star rider. She'd won ribbons and trophies at shows and junior three-day events all over New England. But she'd only been riding again for a month, and so far the only jump Liz allowed her to take was the lowly crossrail.

Holly sighed and adjusted her crash helmet.

The trail narrowed. Kate eased back and let Holly take the lead because she knew these woods better than Kate did. Now and then, there was a break in the trees, and Kate looked up at the mountain towering above them. Ski trails, fresh with summer grass, spilled from its peak like dribbles of green paint. She'd never learned to ski, but if she was still around after the first snowfall, maybe she'd give it a try. Nathan had promised to teach her ... that is, if he ever got back east for another visit. He grew up here, but his entire family now lived in California.

Ahead of her, Holly halted abruptly. "I think I'm lost."

Kate pulled her scattered wits together and looked around—dense woods on both sides, a crumbling stone wall covered with vines, and an odd-shaped tree stump that looked vaguely familiar. Buccaneer had shied at it when they were out looking for Magician.

"This trail leads to the other side of the mountain," she said. "I'm sure of it."

"You mean the place where you found Magician?" Holly said.

"Yeah," Kate said. "I *think* so."

"Then let's go and see if that horse is still there."

Kate urged Rebel into a trot, her mind a whirlwind of events that led her to the mysterious brown mare. Three days before Kate's stunt-double ride, Magician had disappeared. A massive search was organized, and Kate finally found him on the far side of Timber Ridge Mountain. He was locked in a field with a scruffy brown mare that belonged to a crazy old man who lived in a shack. He'd brandished a shotgun and almost pulled Kate off Buccaneer as she led Magician to safety.

They'd called the police, who were supposed to take the old man into custody, along with his brown horse, but they never heard any more about it.

"How much farther?" Holly called back. She was already several lengths ahead, plunging deeper and deeper into the forest.

Kate had no idea. "Ten minutes, I guess."

The trail forked. They took a right, rode down a steep hill and waded through a narrow stream littered with rocks and small branches. Then came another hill. The trail curved to the left, and Kate could finally see the old man's shack ahead of her. It was just the way she remembered—peeling paint, broken windows, and a tin roof that looked ready to collapse. Wisps of smoke curled from a rusty pipe which meant the old man, or somebody else, was still there.

"Be quiet," Kate warned. "Someone's at home."

"I thought the police had arrested him," Holly said.

"So did I."

Holly gave a nervous giggle, and Kate caught her breath, hoping the old man wouldn't come out. They crept past his shack as quietly as they could, keeping their horses on the grass and weeds that edged the rocky trail.

Beyond the old man's house was the field where Kate had found Magician. It was full of junk cars, old tires, and garbage bags spewing rubbish. A half dozen chickens scratched in the dirt; a scrawny goat chewed on a clump of dead thistles.

In one corner stood the derelict shed where the

brown mare lived. Poor thing. Was she still in there? Her mane had been full of knots, her hooves over-grown, and her coat so filthy it was impossible to tell what color she was beneath all the grime. Kate couldn't begin to understand why the awful old man owned a horse. He'd probably stolen her, the way he stole Magician.

"Is this it?" Holly said in a stage whisper.

Kate nodded and stood up in her stirrups, hoping to catch a glimpse of the mare. But there was no sign of her, not even fresh manure. Magician gave a loud neigh, as if he remembered his old pasture mate.

"Sshh," Holly warned. "You'll get us in trouble."

"Wait here," Kate said. "I'll go and look." She dis-mounted and handed Rebel's reins to Holly. Then she hauled herself up the wooden fence, barbed wire snag-ging her breeches. She yanked herself free and dropped to the other side.

An old bathtub, full of scummy green water, had a dead rat floating in it. Kate shuddered. No animal would drink out of *that*. Cautiously, she approached the shed and peeked inside. Dusty cobwebs hung from the rafters, and a gazillion flies swarmed around a loaf of moldy bread; otherwise, the shed was empty. Kate looked around the field again. It wasn't very big. There was nowhere for a horse to hide.

"She's not here," Kate said, running back to join Holly.

"Are you sure?"

"Of course I am." Kate scrambled over the fence, took her horse's reins, and climbed into the saddle. "She's gone."

"Maybe the horse rescue people took her away," Holly said, "like they promised to." She gave a little gulp. "Or she went to the auction."

That's what Kate was afraid of. When it came to horses nobody wanted, auctions were one-way streets to the slaughterhouses in Mexico and Canada. The rescue farms couldn't take them all in. They did their best, but there wasn't nearly enough money to save all the horses that needed saving.

"Come on, let's go," Kate said. "But be quiet. He'll come out and—"

"Too late," Holly said, pointing. "Look."

The old man staggered down his front steps and ran toward them. "Get off my land," he yelled. "You're trespassing!"

Spittle flew from his mouth, and his eyes bulged with anger. He clutched a beer can in each hand. At least he didn't have a gun this time. Rebel spun around like he wanted to bolt. Kate pulled him back to face the old man. Her words spilled out before she could stop them.

"Where's your horse?"

"Kate," Holly yelled. "Don't talk to him!"

But all Kate could think about was the mare's pitiful whinny when she'd taken Magician away. "What have you done with her?"

"What's it to you?" the man said.

He stood about ten feet away, swaying like he was drunk. Kate knew he couldn't run fast enough to catch them, but all the same, he was scary looking with his unshaven face, bare feet, and filthy overalls.

Kate plucked up her courage. "Where is she?"

"Gone," the old man said. "I sold her. Now get out of here before I call the cops." He staggered forward, reaching with bony fingers toward Rebel's bridle.

But Holly got there first. She grabbed Kate's reins and yanked Rebel forward. In a few strides they were clear and the old man was left in the dust, staggering backward and cursing loudly.

"Phew," Holly said, when the old man's shack was behind them. "That was a close one." She slowed her horse and rounded on Kate. "What were you thinking, talking to him like that? Are you totally mad?"

"Yeah," Kate said, feeling stupid.

Holly's voice softened. "Look. We're okay and the horses are okay, so let's go home." There was a pause. "And let's not tell Mom about this."

19

Kate nodded. No way did she want Liz to know she'd just pulled a bone-headed maneuver and almost gotten them in trouble.

* * *

An hour later, Liz met them at the barn. "Hurry up and put your horses away," she said. "I have an idea for Kate."

"Wow, Mom," Holly said. "What it is?"

"I'll tell you later, when you're finished with chores."

Kate tried to keep calm. She took off Rebel's tack and walked him out, then spent a few minutes with Skywalker, Angela's handsome bay gelding. Great whirls of dust dulled his mahogany coat, and his mane sported more tangles than a kitten's ball of yarn. His tail looked even worse.

Gently, Kate wiped mud from his nose and fed him her last carrot when he nuzzled her pockets for a treat. Then she ran down the aisle to join Holly in Liz's office. A mountain of magazines and catalogs spilled from the one extra chair, so Kate parked herself on a pile of horse blankets wedged between a tack trunk and Liz's rusty filing cabinet.

"Make room for me," Holly said. She threw herself down beside Kate. "Okay, Mom. What's the big mystery?"

"No mystery." Liz handed her the local paper, folded open to the classifieds.

Kate blinked. It was the one place they hadn't tried. Holly was so focused on craigslist and horses-for-sale websites that they'd overlooked the obvious.

"Where, Mom?" Holly said. "I don't see it."

"Down there, at the bottom of the page."

"Rowley's Consignment Sale," Holly read out. She frowned. "Mom, what does *consignment* mean?"

Kate read the fine print. "It's an *auction*."

"Ugh," Holly said. "They're awful."

"Not this one," Liz said. "It's a *consignment* auction. The owners place their horses for sale and take them back if they don't sell. The auction's fairly new, and the Larchwood trainer recommended it. He said they usually have quite a few good horses."

"Or a few cans of dog food," Holly muttered.

Kate dug her best friend in the ribs. "Liz, can we go?"

So far, her search had come up with zilch. That morning, before their ride, Kate had checked her own *horse wanted* ad. The only replies were for two yearlings, a sway-backed mare, and an aged Connemara recovering from laminitis.

"Yes," Liz said. "It's on Saturday night, and if you like, we'll have dinner out first, then hit the auction."

"Will they sell other stuff besides horses?" Kate said.

"Yes," Liz said. "They'll have saddles and bridles, halters and hoof dressing, and every sort of pitchfork you can imagine. I need more blankets for the winter, and we could sure use some extra buckets." She sighed. "Skywalker chewed a hole in his."

Holly snorted "*Big* surprise!"

"He's bored witless," Kate said, wondering why Angela even had a horse. She only rode Skywalker when people were watching or when there was a show to get ready for. Apart from that, she hardly went near him.

"Mom, can we afford a new browband for Magician?" Holly said. "The Olympic horses had some really cool ones."

"Tiaras," Kate muttered.

They'd gotten up early to watch the events from London, and Holly had swooned over the dressage horses and their fancy, V-shaped browbands. Some were even studded with crystals.

"I just *love* them," Holly said, shoving Kate sideways.

Liz rolled her eyes. "Okay," she said. "I'll add it to the list." She scribbled on a notepad, then fixed her blue eyes on Kate. "I don't want to interfere, but have you told your father you're planning to buy a horse?"

Kate hesitated. "Not yet, but I'll e-mail him tonight."

"He's in the jungle, remember," Holly whispered. "No Internet."

"Dad won't mind," Kate said, sounding way more confident than she felt. "He loves animals, especially horses."

In reality, Dad had never paid much attention to her passion for horses. *His* passion was butterflies. If a critter had compound eyes, colorful wings, and fuzzy legs, he was all over it. And if Kate told him she had enough money to buy a horse, he'd probably say, "That's nice, dear," then regale her with details about his latest discovery or a scientific paper he was writing.

Her father taught entomology at UConn, and they lived on campus in a tiny condo with a garden the size of a postage stamp. There wasn't enough room for a hamster, let alone a horse. Kate was counting on her old riding teacher, Mrs. Mueller, to give her a job at the barn so she could pay for it all.

* * *

On Saturday afternoon, Kate and Holly swept out the barn's horse trailer. They hosed down the floor mats, filled a haynet with fresh timothy, and rolled up a set of shipping bandages. Kate grabbed a faded green halter and lead rope from the tackroom.

"Gross," Holly said, shaking her head.

Kate looked at the halter. There was nothing wrong with it, except for being a bit frayed at the edges. It belonged to Buccaneer and was left behind when his owner took him away.

"Your new horse needs a new halter," Holly went on.

"Why?"

"Trust me, okay?" Holly struck a pose. "Gray horses look fabulous with purple," she said, flashing hot pink fingernails, "and red is best for bays. Then there's blue for chestnut and emerald green for black and dark brown."

"What about a buckskin?" Kate said. "Or an Appy?"

"I can't see you buying a beige horse," Holly said with an elaborate sigh, "or a spotted one, either, for that matter."

So Kate pulled a couple of twenties from her piggy bank and stuck them in her wallet. She knew better than to argue with Holly when it came to fashion—even horse fashion. Perhaps if she had enough left over, she'd buy a set of matching leg wraps once they found the right horse and Holly told her how to accessorize it. Liz said she'd write a check for the auctioneer, and Kate could pay her back on Monday when the bank opened.

3

KATE WAS SO EXCITED she could barely finish her dinner, even though it was her favorite—pepperoni pizza with mushrooms and extra cheese. All she could think of was the horse she was going to buy at the auction.

As they ate, Liz explained how this consignment sale worked. "All the horses will have a price listed in the catalog," she said. "It'll be the lowest their owners are willing to take. Then it's up to the auctioneer to drive the bidding as high as he can because he gets a percentage of the sale."

"What happens if nobody bids?" Holly said.

"Or they bid, but it's too low?" Kate chimed in.

"Then the horse is withdrawn from the sale," Liz said. "That's why it's different from a regular auction."

"Will they have a horse for me?" Kate said.

"I hope so," Liz said. "But whatever you choose, we need to look it over carefully before bidding."

Kate pushed her empty plate away and glanced at her watch. In another couple of hours she might be the proud owner of a sparkling gray or a brilliant chestnut with a white star and four white socks. She'd even settle for a pinto, if it was as cute as the one that belonged to Adam. He rode for the Larchwood team, one of Timber Ridge's fiercest rivals. His half-Arabian, Domino, was brilliant at dressage and practically unbeatable in the show jumping ring.

Finally, Liz finished her coffee and paid the bill. The auction barn was only a ten-minute drive from the center of Winfield. As they approached it, Kate's excitement rose. So did Holly's, but that was mostly because Adam had promised to meet them there.

Kate nudged Holly. Holly nudged her back.

They both knew what the other was thinking. Kate hugged herself and felt warm inside. She'd never had a best friend before meeting Holly, and now she couldn't imagine life without her.

The parking lot overflowed with trucks and trailers, and Liz had trouble finding a space. With great skill, she maneuvered her rig into a narrow slot between a goose-neck and a four-horse van. On their way to the auction barn, Kate noticed an old cattle truck with slatted sides parked by the fence. A strong smell of cow manure wafted out.

"The kill wagon," Holly muttered.

Kate gulped. "It can't be," she said, feeling sick. "Your mom said this auction was different."

"Then it probably belongs to a farmer with cows," Holly said. "Or pigs." She wrinkled her nose. "It smells bad enough for pigs."

They caught up with Liz inside the barn. The auction ring took up most of the middle, with a line of bleachers down one side. Facing it was a podium and microphone for the auctioneer. Two loudspeakers hung from a beam overhead.

Liz handed the girls a sales sheet, and Kate's hopes faltered as she scanned the list. Only two horses had a starting price she could afford.

"Number nine looks pretty good," Holly said.

Kate read the description: "Chestnut gelding, sixteen hands, good hunter prospect or trail horse. Ten years old. No vices. Starting price: $2,000."

"Maybe nobody else will want him," Holly said.

Kate glanced at the other possibility. Number three was a gray mare, seven years old and described as a challenging intermediate horse. It had a starting price of $1,600.

"Let's go and check them out," Holly said.

Just then, Adam sauntered up. He tipped his baseball cap to Liz and gave Kate a slap on the back. It looked as if he was going to kiss Holly's cheek, but he changed gears at the last minute and slapped her on the back as well.

"How'd you get here?" Holly said.

Adam held up a set of keys. "I drove."

"Whoopee," she cried. "You passed your test."

"Is your mom here?" Liz said.

"Nope, but she's asked me to pick up a few things." Adam pretended to gag. "Yummy stuff like worming medicine, saddle soap, and fly spray."

"Guess what?" Holly said. "We're buying a horse for Kate."

"Cool," Adam said, grinning.

He took off his Red Sox cap and ran a hand through his streaky blond hair. It flopped over his forehead, just the way Nathan's did. It was the same color, too. They even had the same eyes—mossy green with flecks of gold. According to Adam, he and Nathan used to switch clothes in middle school and confuse their teachers. Kate wished she had known them back then. They sounded like a lot more fun than the guys she grew up with.

"Come on, kids," Liz said. "We'd better hustle. The bidding starts at seven and we've got a few horses to check out. Plus I have to buy buckets and blankets."

* * *

Each stall had a number tacked over it, corresponding to the horse's catalog listing. In the first one stood a black gelding. He had a fine head and a short-coupled back. He was only five years old and he reminded Kate of Buccaneer. He whickered when she laid a hand on his shiny rump. His price tag read, $5,000.

Holly pulled her away. "He's out of your league."

They bypassed stall number two and stopped at the third one. The dappled gray was refined and elegant with small ears and a dished face. Other buyers milled about, looking her over and double-checking their catalogs. With all that interest, Liz said, she'd probably sell for a whole lot more than her asking price.

That left number nine. The chestnut gelding.

He was solid and stocky, with a short tail and enormous hindquarters. And when he turned to look at Kate, she winced. A blaze covered his entire face and he had a distinct Roman nose. To make matters worse, one eye was bright blue and the other was a dark, velvety brown.

"Freaky," Holly said. "He looks like a lopsided cow."

Adam gave a loud *moo* and reminded Kate of the cattle truck parked outside. Maybe that's what this horse had arrived in.

"Stop," Liz said, pushing them aside. "The important thing is whether he's sound or not." She stepped into the stall and ran her expert hands down the gelding's front legs. He nudged her, playfully, then lipped at her hair. He blew gently down his nose and shifted to one side so Liz could examine his gigantic hooves.

"Nice," Liz said. "He's a real sweetheart."

Kate took another good look at him. If he was all she could afford, then an ugly horse with mismatched eyes and a Roman nose that looked like a cow was better than no horse at all.

Liz declared him a keeper and told Kate to bid on him. "But now I need your help," she said. "I want to stock up for the barn."

"Me, too," Adam said, tweaking Holly's ponytail. "Mom will kill me if I don't find just the right hair spray."

Holly smacked him. "*Fly* spray, you idiot."

"Help!" Adam cried. "She's beating me up."

One of the loudspeakers crackled into life. The sale would begin in fifteen minutes. Liz and Adam made a beeline for the vendors selling tack and equipment. Holly started to follow, but Kate pulled her back.

"I wonder what's over there?" she said, pointing to a set of double doors. They were half open and beyond them she could see another barn. It looked smaller and darker than the one they were in. "Let's check it out."

"I wouldn't if I were you, miss," said a voice behind them.

Kate turned and found herself nose-to-nose with a short guy wearing a plaid shirt, cowboy boots, and a battered Stetson. A splotchy red birthmark covered half his face. "Why not?" she said, trying not to stare.

"That's where they keep the other horses."

"What *other* horses?" Holly said.

"Rejects," the man said. "But they're in bad shape. There's nowhere else for them to go."

"You mean the dog food factory?" Kate said.

"Yup," the man said, mopping his mottled brow with a blue bandana. "I've been in the horse business for thirty years, and it still bothers me."

Kate was about to ask how many horses were in that other barn when Liz yelled at them to hurry up. She needed help dragging all her stuff to the truck and if they didn't get a move on, they'd miss the opening bids.

* * *

First up was the handsome black gelding, and he sold for seven thousand dollars. The next horse, a bay two-year-old with spindly legs, went for thirty-five hundred, and Kate began to get anxious. These horses were selling for a whole lot more than she had in her savings account.

"Here she is," Holly said, as the gray mare made a

grand entrance. Nostrils flaring, she trotted up and down, tail flagged and ears pricked.

"She's got Arabian blood," Liz said.

The audience applauded as the mare's handler showed her off. She wore a fine show halter and seemed to love the attention. She even let off a couple of playful bucks. But the auctioneer, a robust man in a bright yellow vest, couldn't seem to get anyone to start the bidding.

"Hold up your arm, Kate," Liz said.

"Will I get her for sixteen hundred?"

"Yes, if nobody else bids, so hurry."

Feeling awkward, Kate lifted her arm. It was like being in school and asking permission to go to the bathroom. The auctioneer's wary eyes spotted her immediately and announced he had an opening bid. Would anyone care to raise it? Someone coughed, but no voices rang out. Kate held her breath. Was it really going to be this easy? The auctioneer waved his beefy hands and rattled off a stream of words, but no other arms went up.

"Going once," he finally barked.

"Going twice," he said, and glanced around the audience.

"She's yours," Holly squealed.

Kate's imagination ran wild. Closing her eyes, she dreamed of Holly helping her choose the right shade of purple for her horse's new halter. She'd even allow Holly to talk her into buying one of those fancy browbands because they really were kind of cool, even if they had stupid crystals, and—

"Seventeen fifty," a deep voice rang out.

Kate's eyes snapped open. She looked up and down the bleachers but couldn't figure out where the voice came from. Liz nudged her.

"Eighteen hundred," Kate yelled, raising her arm.

"Nineteen," said a man two rows in front.

"Two thousand," Kate shot back.

But, within a few seconds, the bidding took off and smashed Kate's daydream to bits. Number three sold for five thousand to a woman Liz knew who bred half Arabians.

"That gray's a lovely mare," Liz said. "And she'd make a fine dressage horse, but probably not a good eventer. Not enough bone." She patted Kate's arm. "Hang in there. You have another chance."

"The cow horse," Holly whispered. "Mom said he's really sweet, and he's got plenty of bone. I bet he could jump over these bleachers in a single leap."

Kate faked a smile and wished the chestnut gelding wasn't so ugly. Of course, nobody was forcing her to buy him, but she was getting desperate. The riding team's next event was the charity horse show on Labor Day weekend, and Kate wanted to be in it, riding her own horse and beating Angela Dean fair and square. She wouldn't let Angela cheat her way into the blue ribbon this time.

Five more horses took the spotlight. Then, finally, it was number nine's turn. Laughter rippled through the audience.

"He oughta be in a cattle auction," a shrill voice rang out.

"Or a zoo," said another.

Kate felt instantly sorry for him. The minute the auctioneer opened the bidding, she held up her arm.

"We've got a two thousand bid," the auctioneer said. "This horse is worth twice that, so let's get him moving, folks."

"Twenty-two," said a voice behind them. Kate turned. It was the guy in the plaid shirt. He smiled and nodded at her.

Liz said, "I'll lend you some money if you really want him."

The homely chestnut stood quietly, as placid as a cow, oblivious to taunts and jeers and lazily swishing his stumpy tail. But Kate couldn't go through with it. No matter how good-natured this horse was, he'd always be an ugly horse and she'd probably end up hating him.

"Thanks, but—"

Someone else bid twenty-five, and the chestnut gelding finally sold for thirty-six hundred to the man in the plaid shirt. He stood up and waved his Stetson. "I'm an ugly guy, and I got me a horse to match."

His buddy cheered. "Way to go, Earl. You'll be spoiling that horse to death, just like you do all the others."

The audience whooped and hollered, and Kate let out a sigh of relief. It seemed that the cow-faced horse had found a good home.

Liz yawned. "It's been a long day, and I'm ready to leave."

"Mom," Holly said. "Can't we hang out a bit longer?"

"Ten minutes," Liz said, checking her watch. "I'm off to find coffee. I'll meet you at the truck."

"Adam could bring us home," Holly said.

"Sorry," he said. "I'm not allowed to drive anyone else for another six months. State law."

"Then come and look at tack with me," Holly said. "I'm gonna get a new browband for Magician." She grinned at Kate. "A sparkly one."

Kate shook her head. All the fun had gone out of her evening, and she felt like a fifth wheel. After Holly and Adam took off, Kate slouched along the line of half-empty stalls. She stopped to say goodbye to the cow-faced horse, who was being buckled into a hand-tooled leather halter by his new owner. On the cheekpiece was a brass nameplate that said *Pardner*.

"That's a great name," Kate said.

The man tipped his hat. "Ayuh, and I got me a great horse to go with it." He buffed up the brass plate with his bandana. "It's what I call all my best horses."

Kate trudged on, hands in her pockets and not paying much attention, until she heard voices. They were muffled but loud and seemed to be coming from the small barn. One of the voices belonged to the auctioneer. Looking left, then right, she slipped through the double doors. A weak light bulb, shrouded by cobwebs, hung high in the rafters.

It took a moment for her eyes to adjust. She blinked, and the auctioneer's yellow vest swam into view, brighter than a roll of crime-scene tape. He was arguing with two other men.

Several horses, tied to a rail, jostled for position over a pile of hay. The auctioneer held onto another. Kate blinked again, trying to make out the details. Something swooped past her face, and she almost screamed. A bat, probably.

"You're a *thief*," said a gruff voice. "I'll give you two hundred and not a penny more."

"Three," the auctioneer said.

"Two-fifty."

"Deal!" The auctioneer clapped the other man on the back. Then he held out his fist, and Kate saw money change hands. The auctioneer turned, and Kate shrank into the shadows. He walked right past her, whistling off key, with another man trailing behind.

Kate shook her head, trying to banish the nightmare of dog food cans, all lined up neatly on supermarket shelves. She was about to slip back into the bigger barn when a familiar whinny stopped her cold.

"Come on," said a gruff voice. "I haven't got all night."

Kate froze. That pathetic whinny, the auction, the kill truck outside. They fitted together like a gruesome jigsaw. Swallowing hard, Kate crept from her hiding place. The man and his horse had vanished but they couldn't have gone far.

She had to find them before it was too late.

4

SHADING HER EYES AGAINST HEADLIGHTS, Kate zigzagged across the parking lot. Horns blared; trucks and horse trailers rumbled past. She dodged a departing SUV and narrowly missed being run over by a motorbike. Her foot caught on a rock and over she went, sprawling into a pile of moldy hay.

For what seemed like hours, but was probably only a moment or two, she lay there, head spinning. Someone flopped down beside her.

"Kate, we've been looking *everywhere* for you."

"Phew," Kate said, breathing hard. "You scared me to death."

"Well, you scared *me*," Holly said. She brushed dirt and leaves off Kate's sweatshirt with her baseball cap, then stuck it back on her head. "Where have you been?"

Adam bent down to help her up. "Are you all right?"

"Yeah," Kate said, scrambling to her feet.

"Good," Adam said, "because I gotta run. I'm not supposed to be driving after ten." He gave Holly a double fist bump. "Don't lose her again, okay?"

"I won't." Holly reached for Kate's hand. "Let's go. Mom's waiting."

There wasn't time to explain. Kate shook herself free and raced toward the cattle truck. Its bald tires spun in the dirt as it backed away from the fence. In a moment, it would be gone. She practically threw herself at the driver's door. The smell of manure made her gag.

"Stop!" she yelled. "Slow down."

The driver stuck his head out. A cigarette stub dangled from his mouth. His beady eyes gleamed; his face was dark and narrow, like a weasel. Kate grabbed the truck's wing mirror and held on with both hands. If he drove off, he'd have to take her with him.

"What do you want?" he snarled.

She sucked in her breath. "Did you just buy a horse?"

"I bought six. Now get out of my way, or I'll run you over." He gunned the engine.

"Please," Kate said, "please stop. I need to see them."

The man threw his cigarette out the window and slammed on his brakes. The truck lurched forward, then

39

jerked to a halt, shaking Kate free of the mirror. "What's it to you?"

"I want—" Kate began, searching frantically for a plausible excuse. "I might want to buy one."

"Yeah, right," he sneered. "You gonna bust open your cute little piggy bank and give me all your dimes and quarters?"

Kate shuddered. "Let me just look at them, okay?"

With a muttered curse, the man banged open his door and climbed out of the cab. He glared at Kate, then yanked at the bolts that held the ramp in place.

Holly ran up. "Kate, have you gone totally mad?"

The ramp slammed down with a thud. "There, are you satisfied now, little girl?" he said and lit another cigarette. His match flared briefly, like a miniature torch.

In that instant, Kate counted six horses. Three in front, three behind. Head to tail, jammed in like sardines. The one in the middle, facing her, let out a terrified whinny.

"It's *her*," Kate said. "I knew it."

Weasel Man pushed her aside. "Now, if you've finished gawking at my horses, I wanna get out of here." He bent to lift the ramp, but Kate jumped onto it. Holly jumped up as well.

"What's going on?" Holly asked, wide-eyed.

"I've got to buy her," Kate said, stroking the mare's

filthy nose. The horse trembled but couldn't pull away because she was stuck tight between two sets of hindquarters.

"Why?" Holly said. "She's ten times worse than the cow horse."

"She's not," Kate said. "She's the old man's brown mare."

Holly's mouth fell open. "But—"

"Don't argue," Kate said. "Go and find Liz."

For once, Holly didn't put up a fight. She leaped off the ramp and disappeared in the dark. Now all Kate had to do was keep weasel man talking and prevent him from driving off.

"I'll give you a hundred dollars for her," she said, heart thumping like sneakers in a dryer. "In cash."

"Forget it," he said and rattled the bolts as if he wanted to raise the ramp and lock Kate inside with his horses. He shot her a feral smile. One of his front teeth was missing. "I just paid five hundred for this mare, and—"

"Liar," Kate said. "It was two hundred and fifty." She bit down hard on her fear and looked around for Liz, for anyone who'd help. But nobody stopped. Headlights bounced past her like a video game gone berserk.

"You're wasting my time," the man snapped. He grabbed Kate's arm and tried to pull her off the ramp. In a panic, she reached for the mare's halter. A strap broke, and Kate grabbed another.

"Take your hands off her, Jake Burton."

Liz stormed up the ramp and punched him in the nose. He staggered backward, mouth working furiously like he was trying to spit out a wasp. Liz raked him with her flashlight. "I see you're up to your old tricks again."

Holly gasped. "Mom, do you *know* him?"

"Everyone knows Jake Burton," Liz said. "He's a crook."

All of Kate's bravado fizzled out. She let go of the mare's broken halter and leaned against the wall. Legs trembling, she heard Holly's mom give Jake Burton a verbal tongue lashing. Liz accused him of sneaking around at auctions and buying horses nobody else wanted so he could sell them to the slaughterhouses in Canada.

"Someone's got to do it," he whined.

"Yes, but they've got licenses," Liz said. "And you don't."

"I do," he said.

"So prove it," Liz said. "Show me your license."

For a moment, he did nothing; then he shrugged and kicked childishly at a clump of manure. It splattered all over Kate's sneakers.

"How much did you pay for this horse?" Liz demanded.

"Two hundred and fifty," Kate said. Jake Burton shot her a venomous look.

"And how much could you have sold her for?" Liz said.

His beady eyes gleamed with greed. "Five hundred."

"Horse feathers," Liz snapped. She fumbled in her purse and pulled out a roll of twenties, then pinned Kate with a look. "Are you sure about this?"

"Yes," Kate said, with a vehemence that shocked her. She'd set her heart on finding the perfect horse. Yet here she was, buying a filthy brown mare from a crooked horse dealer.

"I'll take four hundred and not a penny less," he said.

"Two-fifty," Liz countered. "And I won't tell the police about your illegal activities."

"Done."

He snatched the bills from Liz's hands, shoved them into his back pocket, and released the mare's rope. Kate grabbed it before he could change his mind. She half dragged the mare down the shallow ramp. Jack Burton elbowed her out of the way and slammed it shut.

"Mom, you did it!" Holly squealed.

Liz patted the mare's neck. "And goodness knows why."

Kate kept a wary eye on Jake Burton as he scrambled into his truck and drove off. If only she could've rescued the other horses as well. But Liz assured her that she'd call the authorities and let them know what was going on.

"In the meantime," she said, looking at Kate's pathetic new horse, "you've got your work cut out for you." There was a lengthy pause while she felt the mare's legs and examined her teeth.

"What do you think?" Kate said, crossing her fingers. More than anything, she wanted Liz's approval. She wanted Liz to tell her this horse was a treasure, that she'd carry Kate to the Young Rider competition and beyond.

Instead, Liz gave a deep sigh. "If you want my honest opinion, then—" She shook her head, as if searching for the right words. "Kate, I'm sorry, but this mare is a charity case. I suggest we clean her up, put a little meat on her bones, and sell her to someone who just wants a pasture pet. She'll never amount to more than that, I'm afraid."

Disappointment burned its way down Kate's throat. She didn't want to argue with Liz over this. Right now, she had to be grateful that Liz had helped her rescue the mare. Fighting back tears, Kate walked toward the Timber Ridge trailer. The mare shuffled along beside her but balked when she saw the ramp.

"Get some hay," Liz said. "Or a carrot."

Holly jumped into the trailer and snatched a handful of hay. She held it just out of reach. The mare stuck out her nose and sniffed it. Gingerly, she put one hoof on the ramp, then the other. Liz gave the mare a gentle shove from behind and she lurched into the trailer.

"Good girl," Kate said, tying her up.

Under the trailer's dome light, the mare looked even worse than before. In addition to the layers of dirt, she had bug bites on the inside of her ears and they were red and raw. Kate held up a bucket of water and the mare gulped it down like she'd had nothing to drink for days.

"Not too much at once," Liz warned.

Kate dipped her hand in the bucket and wiped the mare's dingy forelock. To her surprise, a hint of silver appeared. Startled by her discovery, Kate rubbed at a patch of mud and dead hair on the mare's shoulder. She wet her hand again and rubbed a bit more, then realized the horse's coat wasn't brown.

It was a bright, coppery chestnut.

5

MAGICIAN GAVE A SOFT NEIGH when he saw his old pasture-mate. "He remembers her," Holly exclaimed. She left Kate holding her bedraggled new horse and ran toward her own.

Kate tightened her grip on the mare's grubby halter. All of a sudden, the barn felt different. Yet nothing had changed. The same horses occupied the same stalls. Familiar rakes and pitchforks hung on the walls, and the orange muck bucket Kate had emptied that afternoon still sat outside Magician's stall. But now, standing beside her very own horse—even if she was a total wreck—Kate knew that something had shifted. She'd crossed some sort of invisible line.

"Liz, where should I put her?" she said.

Liz pointed toward an empty stall across the aisle

from Magician. The stalls on either side were empty as well. "That'll do for now," she said.

Magician neighed again and stretched his velvety black nose over the door as far as it would reach. "He wants to kiss her," Holly said, grinning at Kate. "Let's put her in his stall for the night."

"No way," Liz said. "Kate's mare needs to be isolated. No contact with the other horses till the vet's checked her out."

"Only kidding, Mom," Holly said.

Kate led the nervous mare past Magician and into her new home. Compared to the sleek, well-groomed horses that lived at Timber Ridge, she looked shabbier than ever. Kate's hands itched for a dandy brush and a rubber curry comb to begin cleaning her up. She asked Holly to fetch her grooming box.

"Definitely not," Liz said. "This mare needs time to settle down before you girls smother her with shampoo." She smiled at Kate. "We can't go on calling her 'the mare' forever. Even if you're not going to keep her, she needs a name."

Holly pulled out her new browband and held it against the mare's forehead. It sparkled like a beauty queen's tiara. "How about Princess or Tinkerbell?"

"More like Cinderella," Kate said, gloomily. She scraped another clump of gray mud off her horse's other shoulder. There was no sign of the chestnut hair she'd uncovered earlier, nor of the silvery streaks in the mare's forelock.

She must have imagined them.

"Hold still," Holly said. "And smile. You're supposed to be happy." She snapped a picture with her iPhone before Kate had a chance to object.

* * *

Kate slept badly and woke up late. It was almost ten by the time she and Holly reached the barn. Liz was in the outside ring with a group of beginners.

"I called the vet," she said, as the girls rushed by.

Kate skidded to a halt. "She's okay, isn't she?"

"Yes, but your horse needs shots and check-up," Liz said. "And don't forget to call the farrier. His number's on the bulletin board in my office."

"Thanks," Kate said, feeling guilty. She ought to have been here by six, feeding and grooming her new horse instead of lolling about in bed. She ran to catch up with Holly.

"Oh, no." Holly halted in the barn's doorway.

Kate bumped into her. "What's wrong?"

"Angela," Holly said.

Why did she have to show up today of all days? Angela hadn't been near the barn in weeks. Yet, there she was, standing outside Magician's stall with a girl who could only be her cousin.

"Just ignore them, okay?" Holly said.

Kate clenched and unclenched her fists, then forced herself to stroll down the aisle like she was in no particular hurry. It wasn't easy, pretending not to care when all she wanted was to rush into her horse's stall and stay there, like forever.

Instead, she focused on Angela's cousin.

She was blonde and tan and very tall—a reverse image of Angela who was short with dark hair and skin whiter than a movie star's teeth. Both girls wore skinny jeans and black crop tops over sports bras with purple straps. A pearl, or maybe it was a diamond, glinted at Courtney's navel. She whipped off her sunglasses. So did Angela, as if they'd rehearsed it ahead of time.

It stopped Kate dead in her tracks. The cousins had identical eyes—a pale, icy blue—and right now, all four of them were staring straight at her.

"Who dragged *that* into the barn," Angela said. She pointed at Kate's horse.

Holly grabbed a pitchfork and stood in front of the mare's stall like a sentry on guard duty. "She belongs to Kate."

"Oh, really?" Angela drawled. "How interesting."

"Yes, and it's none of your business."

"My mother wouldn't agree," Angela said, examining her crimson fingernails as if they were of utmost importance. "She'll want to know when the barn turned into a home for derelict horses."

"No problem," Holly said, standing to attention. "You can tell her it happened two weeks ago." With a snappy salute, she zoomed in for the kill. "About the time you stopped grooming Skywalker."

A muffled cry escaped from Angela's pouty lips. Her plucked eyebrows shot so far up her forehead that they disappeared beneath her bangs.

Kate bit back a smile. This was Holly at her best. She'd been shooting holes in Angela ever since kindergarten, and Kate couldn't begin to match her. Besides, it wasn't her place. She was a non-person, as far as Angela and her mother were concerned, and whatever she said would reflect badly on Liz and jeopardize her job. She had to keep quiet.

Through slitted eyes, Angela glared at Kate, then at her horse. "That bag of bones doesn't belong here. It belongs in a dog food factory."

"That's what Kate rescued her from," Holly said.

No sooner were the words out, than Holly's eyes opened wide. *I'm sorry*, she mouthed at Kate.

"What a pity," Angela said. "Now Rover won't get his dinner."

Courtney let out a peal of laughter. "Not even a cat could get a decent meal out of that one." She wrinkled her nose. "This place really stinks."

"Not half as bad as you do," Holly snapped.

It looked as if Angela wanted to smack her. But she rounded on Kate instead. "My mother won't stand for this," she said, in a voice close to hysterics. "She's very fussy about the horses we allow at Timber Ridge. We have standards to keep up." With a dismissive flick, she tossed a wave of black hair over one shoulder. "I can't wait till your father gets home and takes you away. Then things can get back to normal around here."

"So you can start cheating again?" Holly said.

For a moment, nobody moved. Kate didn't dare look at Holly because they'd laugh and ruin it all. Then Angela made a choking noise. She stepped backward, trod on a rake, and landed in the orange muck bucket that Kate had emptied the day before.

"Pity it's not still full of manure," Holly muttered.

But Angela didn't hear. She was making too much of a racket, yelling at Courtney to pull her out.

* * *

"Well, that solves one problem," Holly said, the moment Angela and Courtney flounced out of the barn.

"What?" Kate said.

51

"It's obvious Courtney doesn't ride, so you don't have to worry about her stealing your place on the riding team."

"Yeah," Kate said. "But I'm still worried about Mrs. Dean."

"Don't be silly," Holly said. "The old bat can't force you to get rid of your horse."

"But your mom might," Kate said.

It's what had kept her awake half the night. Liz hadn't been impressed with the mare. She'd called her a pasture pet and said the best thing to do was fatten her up and sell her, then Kate could buy a better horse.

"She'd never do that," Holly said. "Trust me."

Kate wanted to believe Holly, but she wasn't so sure. Angela and her mother had pulled all sorts of underhanded tricks in the past. But there was no sense obsessing over it. She had more important stuff to deal with, like gaining her mare's confidence. She slid back the stall door and held out a carrot.

Her mare hesitated, then whuffled it up.

"Good girl," Kate said.

She ran her hands across the mare's filthy back and down her rump. Bits of bedding clung to her tail like Christmas tree ornaments. Both hocks were crusted with manure and one of her hind hooves had begun to crack.

"What are you going to do first?" Holly said.

"I'm going to give her a bath," Kate said, "if she'll let me, and then I'm going call the farrier." She wanted to clean up her horse before anyone came to check her out.

"Want some help?" Holly said. "I love makeovers."

"You bet," Kate said. She fed the mare another carrot, then fastened her into Buccaneer's old halter.

Holly fetched sponges and her grooming box from the tack room. Kate grabbed a couple of empty buckets and led her mare outside. They tied her up beneath a giant maple. Holly whipped out her iPhone.

"You're not gonna text Adam, are you?" Kate said, impatient to get started.

"No, stupid. I'm taking pictures."

"Why?"

"For the makeover," Holly said.

"But she looks *awful*," Kate wailed.

Holly sighed. "That's the whole point. This is the *before* shot. I'll take another when she's all cleaned up."

Leaving Holly to play fashion photographer, Kate dragged over the garden hose. Her mare eyed it suspiciously and let out a neigh.

From the barn, Magician answered her.

"I'll go get him," Holly said, pocketing her phone. "He could use a bath as well."

"Okay, but tie him to the other tree," Kate said. "We can't let them get too close."

With Magician in sight, the mare settled down. Kate worked shampoo into her filthy coat. In less than two minutes, she was grubbier than the mare, with soap scum all over her arms and face.

"We ought to wash Skywalker as well," Holly said, rinsing Magician's legs with the hose. "He hasn't been groomed in weeks."

"He hasn't been ridden, either," Kate said.

"Then Angela will pay for it," Holly said. "He'll go ballistic on her."

"Probably in front of her new trainer," Kate said.

Holly grinned. "That'll impress him."

Using a soft brush, Kate lathered up her horse again. Gently, she washed the mare's face and discovered a white star in the middle of her forehead. The chestnuts on her forelegs were shaped like commas. Kate's anticipation grew as more layers of mud and matted hair washed away.

This was like the gifts her mom used to give her.

First you unwrapped a big box and found a slightly smaller one inside. You tore the paper off that one, only to find another box and yet another, all done up in different colored papers with bows and funny cards. Sometimes there were six or seven boxes to unwrap, until you reached the smallest box of all. It would be wrapped in gold foil and tied with curly gold ribbons, and hidden inside was the very thing you wanted most in the world.

Just one more box to go.

Pretending they were gold ribbons, Kate pulled the knots and tangles from her mare's mane, then washed and rinsed it. She did the same with her tail. Once it was brushed out, it almost reached the ground.

"She's a blonde," Holly exclaimed.

Fact dissolved into fiction, and Kate tumbled backward into the pages of her favorite book about a chestnut mare with a flaxen mane and tail and a girl named Kate who had brown hair and green eyes. Just like she did.

Kate bit her lip, but the tears came anyway. Mom had wrapped that book in gold paper and curly gold ribbons the last Christmas before she died. Holly dropped her brush in the bucket and gave Kate a hug.

"She's beautiful," Holly said, sniffing.

They were still hanging onto each other when Liz walked up. "Good grief," she said, staring at Kate's dripping wet horse. "Is this the same one we brought home last night?"

Too choked up to speak, Kate nodded.

"What do you think, Mom?" Holly aked.

Wiping her face with a rag, Kate held her breath while Liz ran her expert hands down the mare's legs, examined her eyes, and opened her mouth to check her teeth again.

"She's young," Liz said. "No more than five, maybe six." She patted the mare's rump. "And if I'm not mistaken, I'd say there's some good breeding in here."

"Like what?" Holly said, snapping off more photos.

Liz walked around Kate's horse again, studying her from all angles. She ran a hand through the mare's long mane, then held up a strand of her newly washed tail. It glimmered like silver in the afternoon sun. "I'm betting on Morgan," she finally said.

Kate's heart did a double-bump. She'd always loved Morgans. They were America's first breed of horse. They were versatile and good-natured, and they could do everything from pulling a plow to high-level dressage.

"How tall do you think she is?" Kate said.

Liz shrugged. "Let's find out."

Holly ran into the barn and came back with the measuring stick. Gently, Liz placed the horizontal bar on the highest point of the mare's withers.

Holly whistled. "Fifteen-three."

"Big for a Morgan," Liz said. She turned toward Kate. "Have you found a name for her yet?"

"Not really," Kate said. Her track record at naming animals was pathetic. The only one she'd ever owned was a guinea pig she called Frisky. It barely moved.

"Got any ideas, Mom?" Holly said.

Liz tilted her head to one side. "You know," she said slowly, "this reminds me of a pillow my mother found at a tag sale. It was tattered and torn and incredibly dirty. We told her to throw it away, but she ignored us. And it was a good thing she did, because after she had the pillow dry-cleaned and mended, it turned out to be an exquisite piece of needlepoint. A rags-to-riches sort of thing."

"Just like Kate's horse," Holly said.

"Exactly," Liz replied. "And maybe there's just the right name for her hidden in my story."

"Pillow?" Holly said. "Rags?"

Kate pulled a face and threatened Holly with the hose. "What's another name like needlepoint?" She'd never learned to sew, and her father's only domestic skill was pinning dead butterflies to a board.

"There's embroidery and cross-stitch and quilting," Liz said. "And crewel work, of course."

"That's perfect!" Holly exclaimed. "Someone was very *cruel* to her." She danced in a circle, singing, "Cruella de Vil."

This time, Kate nailed her. She ran the hose up and down Holly's bare legs and then sprayed her hair. Holly squealed and yanked the hose from Kate's hands.

"Hey," Liz said, dodging a stream of water. "I think I've got it."

"Got what?"

"A name for Kate's horse," Liz said. "How about we call her Tapestry?"

* * *

Cool name, Nathan texted later that night. He was already in Romania. There was a seven-hour time difference and it was the middle of the night there. He sent her an icon of a yawn.

After a long pause when Kate figured he'd gone back to sleep, more words spilled across her screen. There were lots of tapestries, Nathan wrote, at the castle they were filming in.

Knights, archers, dead bodies, he texted.

Kate shuddered. But that's what old tapestries were—woven pictures of medieval life, and most were pretty gruesome. She'd looked it up online and learned that the most famous tapestry of all was almost a thousand years old. It hung in a museum in Normandy, France. It was called the Bayeux Tapestry.

"Maybe I should add the word *Bayeux* to Tapestry's name," she mused aloud. "But only for horse shows, like when I have to fill out an entry form."

Holly snorted. "She's a chestnut, not a bay."

"That's not the point," Kate said, laughing.

Holly's nose was out of joint because Adam had gone camping in New Hampshire and had no cell service. Not talking to him every five minutes was making her grumpy.

6

KATE HIT THE BOOKS. She devoured every article on training that she could find. She learned that patience was more important than persistence and that baby steps were easier to pull off than big ones.

She took her mare for long walks. At first, Tapestry was scared of almost everything. She shied at ordinary objects like wheelbarrows and trash cans and almost jumped out of her skin when a couple of barn cats streaked beneath her feet.

After the vet gave Tapestry a clean bill of health, Kate turned her loose in the back pasture with Magician. They grazed on lush grass, nose-to-tail, swishing flies off one another's faces.

"When are you going to ride her?" Holly said. She fished out her iPhone and took another photo.

They'd discussed this the night before when Kate realized she had no clue if her mare had ever been ridden. For all they knew, she might never even have had a saddle on her back.

"Don't rush it," Liz said. "You have all the time in the world."

But she didn't. Kate hadn't told Liz yet, but she wanted to ride Tapestry in the show. Holly thought she was nuts but promised not to say a word.

"My lips are zipped," she said.

Eventually, Kate felt confident enough to lunge Tapestry. She taught the mare voice commands, like when to halt and when to move on. Sometimes, her horse did so well that Kate wondered if she was teaching Tapestry anything new or merely reminding her about stuff she'd learned in another life.

"Tapestry's looking good," Liz said, feeding her a carrot. "She'll fetch a good price, and then you can get yourself a horse you really want."

I've already got what I want, Kate said to herself.

Tapestry's golden coat gleamed like polished copper. Her silvery mane and tail sparkled, and her hooves had healed enough to support shoes. She'd filled out and was well on her way to being the horse Kate had always dreamed of. Never in a million years would she let this mare go.

"Have you told your father about her?" Liz said.

Kate felt herself blush. She'd tried to write several times, but so far all her letters and e-mails had wound up in the trash. She knew she was postponing the inevitable, but she was scared. Suppose her father agreed with Liz and insisted she sell Tapestry?

"Well, have you?" Liz said.

In a flash of inspiration, Kate said, "Would you do it for me?" He'd be far more likely to pay attention to Liz than to her.

"What?" Liz said. "Write to your dad?"

"Yes," Kate said, pulling Tapestry closer. She coiled the lunge line and patted her mare. Tapestry gave a little snort and whuffled at Kate's hand, looking for another treat.

There was a moment's hesitation. Then Liz said, "Okay, I'll do it. But whatever he says, you must respect his decision."

Kate nodded. With luck, Liz's letter would take forever to reach her dad. With even more luck, he'd ignore it.

* * *

The next step came two days later, and it wasn't a baby step. Kate held up a fleece pad for Tapestry to sniff. After a few moments, she placed it gently on the mare's back.

Her skin twitched a little, but that was normal. All horses did that. Then came Holly's saddle. Tapestry blew out her gut before Kate even had a chance to do up the girth.

Liz laughed. "Well, she knows about *that* trick."

"Yeah," Kate said, relieved. Tapestry had clearly had *some* saddle training, but she wouldn't know how much till she got on the mare's back.

Holly thrust a package at her. "It's a horse-warming present," she said, taking hold of Tapestry's lead rope. "From Mom and me."

Kate gulped. She wasn't used to this. Gifts from her father usually involved money or a trip to a museum and dinner in his favorite Peruvian restaurant that made her feel slightly queasy afterward.

"Don't just stare at it," Holly said. "Open it."

Kate ripped off the brown paper to find a brand-new bridle with raised stitching, braided reins, and Holly's fancy browband. The buckles shone, and the leather felt buttery soft beneath her fingers. She tried to say thanks, but the words got stuck in her throat. Any minute now she'd burst into tears.

Holly said, "It came with a plain browband, and I figured Tapestry could wear this one for special occasions. You can swap it back if you want."

"Why?" Kate said. "I mean—"

"Magician hated it," Holly said, grinning. "Too girly-girl for him." She paused. "But it's perfect for Tapestry."

There was a clatter of hooves. Three girls rode into the barn and jumped off their horses. Robin Shapiro led her gray mare, Chantilly, into the stall across from Magician. She stuck her head over the door. "Cool browband," she said. "Where'd you get it?"

"The auction," Holly said.

Sue Piretti patted her Appaloosa's neck. "Tara wants one."

"So does Rebel," said Jennifer West, taking off his saddle. Her chestnut gelding gave her a disdainful look.

Holly snorted. "Yeah, right. He's even more macho than Magician. He'd rather die than wear a tiara."

While everyone laughed, Kate looked from one girl to the other. They were all members of Liz's riding team and they were thrilled that Kate now had a horse of her own.

She finally found her voice. "Thank you."

The bridle didn't have a bit. "We'll get you one later," Liz said, "when you figure out which one Tapestry likes best." She waved toward the tack room. "There are plenty of bits to choose from in there, so help yourself and experiment."

"Thanks," Kate said again, feeling suddenly shy. If

this were Holly, she'd be squealing and jumping up and down, hugging everyone. But that wasn't Kate's style. She'd thank Liz and Holly again later, in private.

"Try putting a little weight on her," Liz said.

She held Tapestry's halter while Kate leaned against the saddle—first one side, then the other, putting a little more pressure on it each time.

Tapestry shifted her feet and flicked her tail, but she didn't seem to mind what Kate was doing. In the end, she looked kind of bored with the whole procedure, as if it were old hat.

"I have a feeling she's going to be fine," Liz said. "You can ride her tomorrow. But right now, I need a few things from the village. Do you guys feel like riding your bikes down there? I've got a lesson in ten minutes."

Holly's cell phone chirped.

It could only be Adam. He'd gotten back from camping and was supposed to be working at Larchwood Stables, but he spent most of his time texting Holly. She said he texted while mucking stalls. Kate wasn't too sure about that. You needed two hands to wield a pitchfork.

Holly grinned and Kate felt a pang of envy. Nathan hadn't texted her in weeks. He was probably in some remote part of Romania without cell service, like on a mountain or in a dungeon.

"Sure," Kate said to Liz. "We'll go."

* * *

An hour later, they ran into Angela and Courtney outside the drugstore. The cousins wore matching outfits—hot pink sundresses, pink sneakers, and sparkly pink headbands. They even had pink socks with little pink bobbles at the back.

"The bubblegum twins," Holly muttered.

Angela twirled a lock of black hair. "My mother's going to see Liz today about getting rid of *that* horse."

Holly rolled her eyes. "Stuff it, Angela."

"What a great idea," Angela said. She gave a fake little laugh and put her hand on Courtney's shoulder. "We could mount her stupid head on the wall. Like a moose."

Kate bit back a retort. She hated it that Holly had to fight her battles for her. But if she ever said a cross word to Angela, Mrs. Dean would fly into the barn on her broomstick and put a curse on them.

"Come on, Angela," Courtney said. She twirled her shopping bag. "Let's go home. I want to try out my new nail polish."

They linked arms and sauntered off.

"Don't let her get to you," Holly said.

Kate reached for her bike. "Does she know what Tapestry looks like now? She hasn't been near the barn in weeks."

"Then she'll be in for a surprise, won't she?"

But as they rode back up the hill, Kate could think of nothing else. "If my horse isn't in her stall when we get back, I'll strangle Angela with a pair of her pink tights."

"Stop worrying," Holly said, pedaling ahead. "Mom won't listen to her."

* * *

Mrs. Dean's silver Mercedes was in the parking lot when they reached the barn. The sight of the car set Kate's teeth on edge. It always meant trouble of one sort or another. Her anxiety deepened when she saw Angela and Courtney leaning against the wall across from Liz's office.

From inside came Mrs. Dean's voice, demanding to see Kate's new horse. "Angela says it's a disgrace to the stables."

"Come with me," Liz said.

She guided Angela's mother down the aisle. In her severe black dress and high heels, Mrs. Dean looked as out of place in the barn as a cockroach on a cupcake. They stopped outside Tapestry's stall.

"Who's that pretty little horse?" Mrs. Dean said.

"Mother! How *could* you?" Angela screamed.

Holly snorted and covered her mouth, but a few giggles escaped anyway. Kate caught the amused expression on Liz's face, but she didn't dare say a word or she'd be laughing as well.

"Now, where is Kate's horse?" Mrs. Dean demanded.

"Right here," Liz said. "This is Tapestry."

"But Angela said—" Mrs. Dean's imperious voice faltered as she looked at Liz, then at Kate's new horse.

"Let *me* see her." Angela pushed past her mother.

Her mouth dropped open at the sight of Tapestry's gleaming chestnut coat, her silvery mane and tail. A shaft of light from the window highlighted the dapples on her rump. Kate and Holly couldn't have staged this better if they'd practiced for a week.

In a neutral voice, Liz said, "Perhaps you should come to the barn more often, Angela. Then you'd know what Tapestry looks like now."

"Angela, what's going on?" Mrs. Dean said. "You told me Kate's horse was filthy and nothing more than a bag of bones."

Holly's giggles finally erupted. Somehow, Kate kept hers under control. Mrs. Dean knew nothing about horses and depended on Angela to keep her informed. But this time, Angela's lies had backfired on both of them. There was no way Mrs. Dean could object to Tapestry now.

"Come on, Courtney," Angela said. "Let's get out of here." She glared at her bewildered mother.

For once, Mrs. Dean actually looked embarrassed, but it didn't last long. She pulled herself together, bestowed a frosty look on Liz, and strode from barn wobbling dangerously on her unsuitable shoes. Bits of dirty shavings clung to the back of her dress.

Liz gasped. "Too funny!"

Holly sat down hard on a trunk, helpless with laughter. Kate joined in and felt her tension drain away. With Mrs. Dean's threat to evict Tapestry behind her, she could throw herself into getting ready for the show.

But first, she had to get on Tapestry's back.

* * *

That night, Kate watched Holly work a little magic with Photoshop. She picked out the best shots of Tapestry's makeover and turned them into a collage. She called it *A tapestry of Tapestry*, then posted it to the barn's Facebook page. Within minutes, ten people had 'liked' it.

"Wow," Adam commented.

Jennifer West wrote, "Rebel's in love with her already."

"He'll have to fight Magician for her," Holly wrote back.

Kate wondered if Nathan would leave a comment. He'd warned her that his Romanian Internet service was unpredictable. Maybe that's why she hadn't heard from him lately.

7

VINCENT KING STROLLED INTO THE BARN at noon the next day. Angela followed, wearing spotless white breeches and a yellow shirt. Her little sister Marcia had been hard at work all morning grooming Skywalker, but Angela kept her distance. She hated getting dirty.

Kate stole a glance at the new trainer.

He was indistinguishable from several others she'd known—whippet thin, with nondescript hair, watchful eyes, and a weather-beaten face that would blend easily into a crowd of horse people. He wore scuffed riding boots, a denim shirt, and tan breeches rubbed thin by years in the saddle—pretty much the standard outfit for trainers everywhere.

It's what Liz always wore. She emerged from her office, said a cheerful hello to the newcomer, and reminded the girls she'd be at a dressage clinic all after-noon. If she was upset over Vincent King treading on her turf, she kept it well hidden.

"I'll be back around six," she said.

Holly led Magician out of his stall. "Mom's given me the go-ahead to practice some bigger jumps," she said to Kate. The black gelding nudged Holly impatiently, as if he couldn't wait to get started. "Wanna come?"

Kate tore her eyes off Angela's trainer. "Yeah."

She tossed the last clump of soiled bedding into a wheelbarrow and pushed it outdoors. Tapestry was in the side paddock, pacing the fence because Magician wasn't in there with her. She paused just long enough to snatch a carrot from Kate's hand.

"I'll come and get you later," Kate promised.

While Holly and Magician warmed up, Kate scurried around the ring. She adjusted oxers and parallel bars, making sure nothing was over three and a half feet. Before her accident two years ago, Holly had jumped much higher. She chafed at the current restrictions, but her mother was adamant.

"Baby steps," Liz kept reminding her daughter.

Ears pricked, Magician cleared the jumps without putting a foot wrong. Holly circled him around and jumped the course again. At this rate, she'd be more than ready for the Labor Day show. Kate glanced toward Vincent King. He was standing by the gate with Courtney, elbows on the top rail, watching them. There was no sign of Angela. She was probably trying to remember how to tack up her horse.

Tapestry, still pounding the fence line, let out a frantic neigh. Head high and tail flagged, she trotted to the center of the paddock.

"Poor thing," Holly said. "She's lonely."

Kate glanced at Vincent King. His attention was now on Tapestry. She neighed again, then charged toward the sturdy fence that separated her from Magician.

"No," Kate yelled. She ran for the gate.

But she was too late.

In one graceful movement, Tapestry gathered herself up and soared over the paddock fence as if it were no higher than the toy jumps in Holly's bedroom. She landed safely and thundered past Kate.

Behind her, someone applauded.

"That mare's a born jumper," said Vincent King. He had a clipped accent, like he was English or maybe a Scot. "Who does she belong to?"

"Me," Kate said, staring at the fence Tapestry had just cleared. It was almost five feet. Even Magician had never challenged it.

"What's her breeding?" the trainer said.

"We're not sure, but Liz thinks she's a Morgan."

"No papers, huh?"

Kate shook her head. Something about Vincent King's eyes bothered her. Not that she could see much of them beneath the brim of his cap. It was the same sort of cap that British trainers wore. It went along with Jack Russell terriers, Land Rovers, and tweed jackets with leather patches on the elbows.

She pulled a carrot from her pocket—thank goodness she had one left—and hurried toward Tapestry. But she needn't have worried about catching her. The mare was happily nuzzling Magician's nose, unaware of the minor panic she'd just caused.

"Well, at least we know she can jump," Holly said.

Kate took her mare's halter. "And how!"

The gate swung open, and Angela rode in. Skywalker jigged about like a nervous two-year-old. He'd already worked up a sweat. Vincent King told her to ride in a circle and within minutes, Kate heard him criticizing Angela's seat, her hands, and the angle of her knee.

"He's gonna barbecue her," Holly muttered, "and in front of her precious cousin, too."

"Makes me feel almost sorry for her," Kate said.

Holly scowled. "I wouldn't go *that* far." She gathered up her reins. "So, what did the great trainer say?"

Still watching Angela, Kate said, "Just that she's a good jumper, and—"

"And what?" Holly prompted.

"He asked who she belonged to."

"Good thing Mom wasn't there," Holly said, with a grimace. "She'd have gotten him to make you an offer."

* * *

Magician's saddle was still warm when Kate took it off and placed it on Tapestry's back. The barn was empty except for her and Holly and their two horses. Sue, Robin, and Jennifer had gone trail riding, and the barn's other horses were in the back pasture. Angela was still outside with her trainer.

Kate slipped the new bridle onto Tapestry's head.

"It suits her," Holly said, approvingly.

While Tapestry chewed at the snaffle Liz had recommended, Kate adjusted the lungeing cavesson and led her mare into the indoor arena. She lined her up with the mounting block and tried not to feel nervous. Suppose they were wrong and Tapestry had never been ridden before, or she had but it was a disaster, and—

"Think we should wait for Mom?" Holly said.

"She won't be back till six, remember?" Kate said. "I want to get this over with now."

"While nobody's watching?"

Kate nodded. "Except you."

"Then let's do it." Holly grasped the reins. "One, two—"

On the count of "three," Kate stuck her foot in the stirrup, swung her leg over Tapestry's back, and lowered herself gently into the saddle. The mare gave a little grunt and shifted sideways, then looked around as if to say, *Okay, now what*?

"So, how does it feel?" Holly said.

For a moment, Kate couldn't speak. Her mind was bursting with far-fetched fantasies—riding Tapestry in the Olympics, winning gold in the three-day event, standing on the podium and—

Holly's voice brought her back to earth. "Well?"

"It's awesome and scary and kind of hard to believe," Kate said. "I think it must be like—" She knew what she wanted to say, but the words got tangled in her tongue.

Holly raised an eyebrow "Like what?"

"The first time you rode Magician again."

"I seem to remember I fell off," Holly said, grinning as she clipped the lunge line to Tapestry's cavesson. "Now, walk on."

Gently, Kate squeezed with her legs. Tapestry moved into a flat-footed walk with a longer stride than Kate expected. After circling Holly for a few minutes, she squeezed again and asked for a trot.

"She's looking good," Holly said.

Tightening her hold on the reins, Kate sat deeper in the saddle. Tapestry responded to her signals like clockwork and swung into a smooth, easygoing canter. Kate's heart did a couple of somersaults. This was finally it. She was riding her very own horse for the very first time, and it was the most dazzling feeling in the world.

"Keep your heels down," Holly yelled.

"You sound like your mother," Kate yelled back.

Another fantasy bloomed. She would take Tapestry to England next summer. She and Holly had been invited to train at Beaumont Park, the famous equestrian center owned by Jennifer West's Olympic grandmother. They had tons of amazing horses there, but she'd much rather have Tapestry. Holly could bring Magician, and—

With a squeal, Tapestry dropped her nose and let out a playful buck. Kate's fantasy flew in one direction and she flew in the other, right over Tapestry's head. She landed in the soft tanbark a couple of yards from Holly's feet.

"Are you all right?" she said, helping Kate up.

Kate pulled a face. "I'm fine, but my ego's broken."

"You should ride that horse in a rodeo," came a scornful voice.

Another voice chimed in. "Or maybe a circus. She'd make a great clown."

Groaning, Kate looked up to find Angela and Courtney, along with Vincent King, leaning on the rail. He tipped his cap at her, then turned around and left. He was, Kate noticed, very slightly bow-legged.

* * *

After Liz got through bawling them out for riding Tapestry without supervision, she calmed down and listened to all the details. "It's obvious she's been well-trained by someone who knew what they were doing," she finally said.

"But who?" Holly said. "That's the big question."

"Here's a bigger one," Liz said. "How did she end up with the old man? Where did he get her?"

"That's easy," Kate said. "He stole her."

"Like he stole Magician," Holly added.

"Okay, girls. Think about it," Liz said. "Tapestry's a well-bred horse. She was grubby and neglected when Kate rescued her, but underneath all the grime, she wasn't in terribly bad shape. Look at how she's filled out in just a few weeks."

"Mom, what you getting at?"

"If she was stolen," Liz said, slowly, "it means somebody is probably looking for her."

Kate gasped. So did Holly. Neither of them had even thought about this. Tears sprang to Kate's eyes. She rubbed them away angrily. She would *not* fall apart. There had to be another explanation. Maybe the old man didn't steal her. Maybe she got loose and he happened to find her, or perhaps he bought her at an auction, just the way Kate did, and—

Holly said, "Tapestry belongs to Kate. She rescued her. If she hadn't, Tapestry would be horse meat by now."

"I agree," Liz said. "Let's hope the law does, too."

"It won't come to that, will it?" Holly said.

Her mother frowned. "I'm not going to say a word about this. But if someone comes looking, we have to be honest."

"Suppose they're crooks, too?" Holly said.

"Then we'll set Aunt Bea on them."

Holly squealed. "Is she coming to visit?"

Liz nodded. "I've invited her to help choose our riding team for the show."

"Mom, that's great, but why?" Holly said. "You always pick the team yourself."

"Not this time, Holly," Liz said. "With you trying out, someone's sure to complain about favoritism."

Holly shrugged. "Aunt Bea will pick me, anyway."

"Probably," said her mother. "But to balance things out, I've asked Vincent King to help."

"Because he'll choose Angela?" Kate said.

At the last show, Angela had cheated her way into the blue ribbon. Kate was determined it wouldn't happen again. She wanted another chance to compete against her unscrupulous rival—and beat her.

"Precisely," Liz said. "And—"

"—Mrs. Dean would kill him if he didn't," Holly finished.

Liz bit her lip. "That's enough, young lady."

"Okay, so when's Aunt Bea coming?" Holly said.

"The end of next week."

Kate's mood lifted. Aunt Bea had a nose for trouble. She wrote mysteries and horse books for kids, and she'd organized the successful search for Magician. She would know just how to solve the problem of whoever it was that once owned Tapestry.

* * *

It didn't take long for Tapestry to catch up with the others. Within a few days, she graduated from the cross-rails and brush jump to the double oxer and parallel bars. Even the forbidding red wall didn't faze her. Her only problem was the coop. She refused to go anywhere near it.

Holly grinned. "She's chicken."

"Not funny," Kate snapped.

She jumped off Tapestry and led her in circles around the coop's wooden A-frame. It wasn't very high or even brightly painted like the other jumps, but Tapestry eyed it warily, as if it had big teeth. There'd been something similar in the old man's field that his scrawny chickens lived in. Maybe that's what was bugging her.

"Don't push it," Liz said, after Tapestry dug her toes in again. "There's never been a coop at this show before."

* * *

While Liz coached her riders in the outdoor ring, Vincent King worked with Angela inside. Sometimes he brought an assistant—a sour-faced woman named Sharon who carried a large canvas bag slung over her shoulder. They would close the arena's sliding doors, shutting everyone out ... including Mrs. Dean.

"It's the way I teach," Vincent said, when she objected.

One afternoon, Kate found Angela in the tack room rubbing soap furiously into Skywalker's saddle. Her shoulders were shaking. Kate was stunned. She'd never seen Angela clean tack before. She'd never seen her cry, either—not even when her mother yelled at her for losing a tennis match the week before.

"Hey, are you all right?" Kate said.

"Go away," Angela said. Her face was paler than ever, her eyes smudged with mascara. She looked like a raccoon.

Kate said. "What's wrong?"

"None of your business." Stifling a sob, Angela abandoned her saddle and raced through the door.

"What was all *that* about?" Holly said, walking inside with two boxes of worming medicine. She dumped them on the floor. "Angela almost ran me over."

"She was cleaning tack."

Holly raised an eyebrow. "You've got to be kidding."

"Nope." Kate pointed to Skywalker's saddle, cleaner than it had been in months. "I guess Mr. King hauled her over the coals for it. He's been on her case about everything else."

The whole barn knew. They'd all heard the yelling and screaming. Vincent King's insults came hurtling through the walls like bullets. A few minutes later, Angela would emerge from the arena looking pale and shaken.

"It's only a local show," Holly said. "Anyone would think he was coaching her for the Medal Maclay."

"Or the Olympics," Kate said.

It was Mrs. Dean's fault. She pushed Angela to win, even if it meant being chewed out by irrational trainers.

Kate shuddered and felt sorry for Angela. Mrs. Dean was the worst kind of horse show mother.

Liz stuck her head around the door. "News flash," she said. "Mrs. Dean's hired a photographer. He'll be here tomorrow to take publicity pictures of Angela and Skywalker."

"Why?" Holly said.

"For the horse show," Liz said. She picked a tarnished curb chain off the floor and stuck it in her pocket. "It's a charity show, remember? And it's for one of Mrs. Dean's favorite causes."

"Yeah," Holly said. "The March of Dimes for Meddling Mothers."

"That's enough," Liz said, pinning Holly with a look. "Just try to be helpful, okay?"

Holly snorted. "Angela hasn't been chosen yet."

"But she will be," Kate said.

Mrs. Dean was probably paying Vincent King a small fortune to make sure of that.

8

MRS. DEAN MADE A GRAND ENTRANCE early the next morning, followed by her photographer and a cartload of equipment. Behind them came Angela, looking sulkier than ever. She was all trussed up in a classical dressage outfit—shadbelly coat, yellow vest, white breeches, and boots that were too tall to walk in. Beneath one arm she carried a black top hat.

Holly groaned. "She's a groom on a wedding cake."

"And here comes the bride," Kate said.

Down the aisle strolled Courtney, looking terminally bored in a white tennis dress, silver sneakers, and silver wristbands. In one hand she held a chrome tennis racket. In the other she twirled a silver iPod.

"Close enough," Holly said, laughing.

Kate felt a tiny bit sorry for Angela. This whole cha-

84

rade was clearly another of her mother's dumb ideas. She'd organized a medieval pageant in July and wanted the riding team to stage a jousting tournament, complete with broom handles for lances and trash-can lids for shields. Liz had firmly, but politely, turned her down.

* * *

By ten o'clock, the barn was in an uproar. The photographer set up his tripod and umbrella lamps outside the tack room, changed his mind, and moved them further down the aisle where they blocked access to the indoor arena. He insisted the splintery old doors made a perfect backdrop. Liz suggested it would make more sense to take Angela's photos outside, but Mrs. Dean overruled her.

"Marcia, hurry up with the horse," she said. "We haven't got all day."

Skywalker's door slid open, and Angela's sister led him into the aisle. She'd polished his hooves and braided his mane, but obviously she hadn't been able to reach his forelock. It flopped messily between his ears.

"I'll do it," Kate offered.

Angela shrugged. "Whatever."

Kate whipped an elastic from her pocket and braided Skywalker's forelock, but only to help Marcia. The poor kid had been working since breakfast to get her sister's horse clean.

It was another twenty minutes before the photographer was finally ready. He shot pictures of Angela alone, then Skywalker by himself, then both of them together. He fussed over the angle of Angela's hat and complained because her horse wouldn't keep still.

Courtney hung about, yawning.

Mrs. Dean patted her arm. "It'll be your turn, soon. We'll shoot you at the tennis club."

"Bang," Holly said.

Kate exploded with laughter. Mrs. Dean glared at her. "If you can't be civil, then please leave."

Stifling their giggles, Kate and Holly retreated to the tack room. Liz had taken the younger kids outside for a lesson; Sue, Robin, and Jennifer had gone trail riding. The barn wasn't quite as chaotic as it had been an hour earlier.

Holly collapsed on a tack trunk. "Good thing Vincent the King isn't here. He'd have a royal meltdown."

"Hush," Kate said, and stuck her head out the door. "Here's Queen Sharon. She can have one for him."

With a curt nod, the trainer's assistant strode past and tried to push her way into the indoor arena, but the photographer stopped her.

"You'll have to wait till I'm finished," he said.

Sharon looked ready to argue but dropped her

canvas bag on the concrete floor with a thud. Sighing, she checked her watch and leaned against the wall.

"I'd love to see what's in that bag," Kate whispered.

Holly joined Kate in the doorway. "Me, too," she said. "But how?"

"Distract her," Kate said. "And I'll take a look. But do it quick before Vincent shows up."

Holly thought for a minute. "Okay, I've got it." She shoved both hands in her pockets and strolled up to Sharon "There's coffee in my mother's office, if you'd like some."

"Yeah, sure," Sharon said. "Where is it?"

"I'll show you," Holly said.

For a moment, Kate thought Sharon was going to pick up her bag. Her hand hovered over its leather handles. Then she shrugged and followed Holly into Liz's office.

Kate darted across the aisle. She had a minute, maybe less if Sharon didn't take cream or sugar in her coffee. The bag's zipper was heavy brass with big teeth, and it had a padlock. Kate's heart sank, but she pulled the zipper anyway.

The bag yawned open.

Inside were two pairs of rubber gloves with long gauntlets. Beneath them, Kate saw two coils of wire, a pack of batteries, and what appeared to be a box with metal clips. It was hard to tell. She zipped the bag shut.

"Looking for something?" said a voice behind her.

Kate did the only thing possible. She fainted at Vincent King's feet.

* * *

Holly heard the commotion and rushed out of her mother's office, with Sharon hot on her heels. Kate was sitting up and groaning, holding onto her stomach. Had Vincent King slugged her, or was she really sick?

"Are you okay?"

"No," Kate gasped. "My stomach is—"

"It's that moldy hot dog you ate last night," Holly said, thinking fast. "I told you it was bad."

Kate retched, convincingly. The trainer stepped back. He shot Holly a penetrating look as if he didn't know what to think and then picked up Sharon's bag. The zipper was closed. Had Kate seen what was in it?

Vincent King nodded at his assistant. "Tell Mrs. Dean we'll skip today's lesson."

Furtively, Holly glanced toward the arena doors. Angela's mother didn't appear to have noticed Kate's dramatic performance. She was too busy telling the photographer how to do his job. Courtney was perched on a metal chair, snapping her fingers and lost in her iPod.

Another groan escaped from Kate.

Maybe she really *was* sick. Holly squatted beside her and waited for Vincent King and Sharon to leave. The moment they disappeared, Kate scrambled to her feet.

"Phew," Holly said. "I figured you had food poisoning. You really fooled me."

"Good," Kate said. "But did I fool Vincent King?"

* * *

"Maybe Sharon moonlights as an electrician," Holly said. "Lots of horse people have two jobs. Mom used to work nights as a waitress before she married my dad."

"So why does Sharon bring her bag into the barn?"

Holly shrugged. "It's too valuable to leave in her truck?"

"C'mon," Kate said. "It's just a bunch of wire, two pairs of rubber gloves, some batteries, and a box with clips on it. So, what's it all worth? Thirty dollars? Forty?"

"I dunno," Holly said. "I never bought any."

"There's got to be another explanation," Kate said. "I guess we could always ask Angela. She's in there with them."

"Drop it," Holly said. "It's none of our business. Besides, we've got the show coming up, and Aunt Bea, and—"

Her iPhone chirped.

"—and Adam," Kate finished, as Holly fled into Magician's stall to chat with her boyfriend in private.

Gloomily, Kate checked her own cell phone. She hadn't heard from Nathan since the night they'd texted about Tapestry's name. No e-mail, no private messages, no tweets. Nothing. He'd dropped off her radar, but he hadn't dropped off Facebook. His fan page was bursting with details about Romania and the castle and Tess O'Donnell, his glamorous co-star.

Kate gave a little sigh.

Nathan's page was orchestrated by his manager and a team of publicists. Nathan had nothing to do with it. Angela had begged him for his private e-mail address, but he'd given it to Kate instead, along with his cell phone number. And then he'd kissed her. She put a hand to her cheek. Holly had told her never, ever to wash it.

But she had to face facts. Nathan Crane was a movie star, a teen idol. He had a bazillion girls swooning all over him. He didn't need plain old Kate McGregor.

Holly's voice wafted toward her, telling Adam about Sharon and her mysterious bag. Jealousy's green fingers tapped Kate on the shoulder. Angrily, she shrugged them off. *Best friends weren't supposed to be jealous of one another, were they?* Kate had never had one before. She didn't know the BFF rules or even if there were any. Tapestry stuck her head over the stall door and whickered softly.

"You're my other best friend," Kate said.

She wrapped her arms around Tapestry's warm neck and felt like she never wanted to let go.

* * *

Photos of Angela sprouted all over the web. Her fake smile appeared on Facebook and Pinterest and on Mrs. Dean's charity site with a link to the state's largest newspaper, where someone, Mrs. Dean probably, had written a gushing article about Timber Ridge's "sparkling young dressage star."

"Some star," Holly said. "Angela doesn't know a flying change from a flying squirrel."

"Or a piaffe from a box of popcorn," Kate said.

She clicked on the barn's Facebook page. Angela's photo showed up there as well, just above Tapestry's collage, and it had a string of comments from people Kate had never heard of. Someone named Richard North wrote, *Nice outfit, but isn't she a bit young to be wearing grand prix clothes?*

"Bingo," Holly said, giving Kate a high five.

Kate grinned. This guy, whoever he was, had nailed it. At best, Angela was a first-level rider, which meant you wore hunt jackets and helmets, not top hats and shadbelly coats. It took years and years of training to reach the heady world of grand prix dressage—and the classical outfits that went along with it.

Leaning over Kate's shoulder, Holly said, "Scroll down. I want to check out Tapestry's comments."

There were now more than fifty. Even Mrs. Mueller, Kate's old riding teacher, had chimed in with, *Spectacular horse, Kate. I'm so pleased for you.* Kate expanded the list. Maybe there was one from Nathan, or even her father. Liz had written to him, but she hadn't heard back.

"Stop," Holly said. "Go up a bit."

"Why?"

"That," Holly said. She jabbed her finger at the screen. "It's the same guy who commented on Angela's outfit."

Richard North had left another comment, this one about Tapestry: *Love to see more photos.*

Kate said, "How many photos do you have?" Holly had been snapping pictures of Tapestry since the day they brought her home.

"Tons," Holly said.

"So let's upload some of them."

"Don't be an idiot," Holly said. "This guy's obviously a creep. He gets his kicks by stalking horses on Facebook."

Kate hadn't thought of that. Facebook was still a bit of a mystery to her. You post stuff, but you don't really know where it goes or where other stuff comes from. Holly teased her about this. A kid who didn't totally get Facebook was a weirdo.

"Check out Angela's page," Holly said. "I want to see if he's posted over there."

But there was nothing from Richard North on Angela's wall. Kate scrolled down. "Oh, no," she said, feeling sick.

Angela had shared Tapestry's collage. Beneath it, she'd written: *Did this horse run away from your barn, or did someone steal it?*

* * *

Just when Kate thought things couldn't get any worse, Aunt Bea called. She wouldn't be able to come and help choose the team. Her publisher had rearranged her book tour schedule and she'd be leaving for Chicago in the morning.

"Now what?" said Kate, when Liz gave them the news.

"It'll be up to Vincent King," Liz replied.

"Mom, isn't there anyone else you could ask?"

"I've already tried," Liz said. "But nobody's available, not on short notice. I need the team all figured out by tomorrow so we can decide the best classes for you kids to enter."

"Jumping," said Holly.

"You have to get chosen first," reminded her mother.

Kate studied the list, but the words swam before her eyes. *Equitation*, *pleasure*, and *hunter* classes melded into a big mess and blurred her vision. There was no sense obsessing about this. Vincent King wouldn't pick her in a million years ... not after the fiasco over Sharon's stupid bag.

"But there is good news," Liz said. "Mrs. Dean has organized a party at the club, and we're all invited."

"Cool," Holly said. "When?"

"Next Friday."

"Two days before the show?" Kate said. How stupid was that? They should be cleaning tack and schooling their horses, not getting all gussied up for a dumb social event.

But Holly refused to back off.

"It's a *costume* party," she said, reading the flyer Mrs. Dean had sent around. "We've got to dress up as a famous rider or as something with the word *horse* in it." She grabbed Kate's arm. "This will be so much fun. I can help you with makeup and your hair and—"

"Waste of time," Kate said.

"Why?"

"Because I'm gonna be the headless horseman."

AT TEN THE NEXT MORNING, Liz gathered her students in the outdoor ring and delivered a last-minute pep talk.

"Okay, girls. I've asked Mr. King to choose three riders for the team events," she said. "It wouldn't be fair for me to do it because Holly's trying out."

Everyone cheered, except Angela.

"But remember," Liz went on. "No matter whom he picks, I think you're all absolutely great."

"Can we still go, even if we're not picked?" Robin said.

"Of course," Liz replied. "This isn't just a show for riding teams. It's for individual riders, as well. You can choose three classes—two serious ones and another for fun, like the sack race or apple bobbing."

"I love apple bobbing," Holly said. "So does Magician. He always gets to the bucket before I do."

"Then you'll have to try harder," Liz said.

With a smile, she walked down the line of riders, stopping to pat each horse. She adjusted Sue's stirrups, wiped grass from Chantilly's snaffle, and told Jennifer to check her girth.

"It looks a little loose," she said.

Kate checked her own, then leaned forward to slide the keeper up Tapestry's throat latch. Vincent King was a stickler about tack. He'd already proved that by screaming at Angela for not cleaning hers. She circled the group on a restless Skywalker. His shoulders were already in a lather, as if he sensed that the demanding trainer was about to show up.

Vincent King arrived five minutes later and told everyone to take the rail. Making notes on a clipboard, he barked out commands for a trot, back to a walk, then a canter.

"I said canter, not gallop," he yelled at Angela.

But Skywalker was out of control. He thundered past Sue and Tara, then plowed into Chantilly who bucked and almost unseated Robin. Her helmet went flying and King hollered at her for not having it fastened securely enough.

The group halted while Robin retrieved her hat.

"Are we having fun yet?" Holly muttered.

Magician snorted and tried to nibble Tapestry's mane. He was much more interested in his girlfriend than in standing still. Sue edged her horse closer to Magician. She glanced at Vincent King, now helping Liz adjust the parallel bars.

"Is he always like this?" she said.

Holly rolled her eyes. "No, he's usually much worse. Haven't you heard him screaming at Angela? I don't know how she puts up with it."

Neither did Kate. It wasn't Liz's style, but she'd read about other trainers abusing their students so badly that they switched trainers or gave up riding altogether.

Vincent King told Angela to jump first.

On a tight rein, she cantered Skywalker in a circle and aimed him at the oxer. He cleared it with two feet to spare, then bounded over the parallel bars like a kangaroo.

"Wow," Sue said. "He's really picking his feet up."

Too much, Kate thought. There was something unnatural about the way Skywalker tucked his front legs under his body as he took the jump—like he was terrified of touching it.

Robin was next in line, and Vincent King told her to take Chantilly over the wall and the crossrail. He appeared to be cherry-picking the jumps. Kate looked at the coop. It would be just her luck if he picked that one for her.

Instead of two jumps, he selected three for Holly.

Magician soared over the double oxer, the gate, and the brush jump with ease. Then Jennifer West took the same ones. As usual, Rebel didn't put a foot wrong, but Sue's mare knocked a brick from the wall and sent rails flying off the hogsback.

"Rotten luck," Kate said.

Sue shrugged. "I'm just glad it's over."

While Liz and Vincent King reassembled the jumps Sue had demolished, Kate took deep, calming breaths. The last thing she wanted was to send her jangled nerves down the reins to Tapestry's sensitive mouth.

The trainer walked up and put a hand on Kate's boot. His fingernails were dirty. "I've seen your horse jump the paddock fence," he said. "Now show me what she can do with you on her back."

"Which jumps?" Kate said.

He gave her a sly smile. "How about the coop and the hogsback? You can throw in the double oxer as well if you really want to impress me."

"But—" Kate said, then clamped her mouth shut.

"Is something wrong?" he said.

She gathered up her courage. "No."

* * *

Kate's stomach tightened into a knot. Urging Tapestry into a canter, she considered her options. It didn't matter what order she took the jumps in. She decided to leave the worst one for last.

Ears pricked, Tapestry pounded toward the red-and-white oxer. Without missing a beat, she leaped over it. The moment they landed, Kate made a sharp turn and aimed for the hogsback—a fearsome spread of three rails, with the middle one higher than the other two. She'd jumped it many times on Magician, but not on Tapestry.

Her mare didn't even hesitate. She flicked her ears, waiting for Kate's signal, then took off like a giant golden bird. In the distance, Kate heard somebody clapping.

"Way to go," Holly yelled.

For a brief second, Kate thought about quitting while she was ahead. What would Vincent King do? Bawl her out for avoiding the coop? Its triangular bulk loomed ominously at the far end of the ring. Slowing to a trot, she caught her breath, and looked at the jump again. It was a stupid wooden box, all of two feet high, with a rustic pole on top. Even Plug, the barn's beginner pony, jumped it.

"We can do it, girl," Kate said.

But Tapestry wasn't listening. She dodged left, then right, like a cow pony herding cattle, and slid to a stop ten feet in front of the jump. She let out a gigantic snort, as if challenging her demons to come out and fight. Kate tried again. Whispering words of encouragement, she guided her mare in a circle and faced her at the jump. This time, they got within sniffing distance before Tapestry dug her toes in.

Kate's confidence vanished. She knew it was hopeless. The minute a rider gave up, so did the horse. No way was Tapestry going to jump the coop. At least, not this morning and not with Vincent King's critical eyes boring into her.

"Okay, that's it," he called out.

Forcing herself to smile, Kate rode back to the group. Vincent King handed his notes to Liz. She thanked him, and he turned around and walked away. Angela shot Kate a scornful look, then followed her trainer through the gate. Clearly, she knew she'd made the team.

It was a foregone conclusion.

* * *

Kate lagged behind the other kids as they headed for the barn. She'd blown it, but who cared? She could still ride in the show, so it really didn't matter.

100

Oh, yes, it did.

This was the last big show of the season. There wouldn't be another chance to compete against Angela on equal terms, in the same events, head-to-head for the blue ribbon.

Maybe she wouldn't even go.

But that would be admitting defeat. Even worse, it would be like slapping her best friend in the face. Holly had spent two years going to horse shows in a wheelchair, watching other girls ride Magician and not even complaining about it.

Kate felt herself blushing with shame.

Liz told everyone to meet her in the tack room after they took care of their horses. Kate dawdled, putting off the inevitable. She removed Tapestry's saddle, threw on a cooler, and walked her mare around the back paddock for ten minutes longer than she needed to. By the time she reached the tack room, the others were already there. Angela stood in the doorway with Courtney. Kate tried to squeeze between them.

With an elaborate sigh, Angela moved over.

Courtney tossed back her hair and wandered off, hitting imaginary balls with her tennis racquet as if she didn't care whether her cousin was chosen. More than likely, she already knew the outcome.

Kate unfolded a metal chair and sat down.

Liz glanced at her notes. "First off," she said. "Mr. King agrees with me. You're all talented riders. He hadn't seen you all in action before, and he was most impressed."

Holly gave a little snort. Liz shot her a warning look.

"Okay, so here's the scoop," she said. "Our team for the show will be Angela—"

No surprise there, Kate thought.

"—and Holly," Liz said.

The girls whooped with delight. Kate gave Holly a double fist bump and glanced at Angela. Her pale face gave nothing away. Only her eyes betrayed a flicker of emotion, but then it vanished as if a curtain had come down. She didn't seem the least bit surprised, or even pleased, to have been picked.

"So who's third?" she said, shrugging.

"Jennifer," Liz replied, "with Kate in reserve in case somebody has to drop out."

"Yeah, like that's gonna happen," Angela said.

Kate bit her lip. She had to be upbeat about this. No way would she give Angela the satisfaction of knowing how crushed she was. Holly shot her a look of sympathy. *I'm sorry*, she mouthed.

Liz handed out prize lists. "We'll sort out the major classes later this afternoon, but right now I'd like you to choose a fun event." She smiled at them. "If you want to."

"I'm all over the egg-and-spoon race," Jennifer said.

"Apple bobbing," Holly said, nudging Kate. "Do it with me. Tapestry will love it."

"I'll try the sack race," Sue said. "I'm good at hopping."

"Me, too," said Robin.

Angela flung down her list. "This is stupid," she said. "It's worse than a field day in third grade."

"Oh, chill out, Angela," Holly said.

Liz stood up. She ushered everyone, except Kate and Holly, into the aisle. Slowly, she closed the tack room door.

"Uh, oh," Holly said. "I smell trouble."

"Liz, what's wrong?" Kate said, antenna on full alert.

Liz looked at her. "Kate, I know you're disappointed about not making the team, and I hate to dump more misery on you, but this has to be dealt with."

"Mom, what is it?"

"I had a disturbing phone call this morning," Liz said. "It's about Tapestry."

"Who from?" Kate said.

"A man called Richard North. He's pretty sure that Tapestry belongs to him."

10

"MOM, THAT GUY'S A CREEP," Holly said. "He's a horse stalker. He left a comment on the barn's Facebook page about Angela's stupid dressage outfit, and then he asked for—"

"—more pictures of Tapestry," Kate finished.

Liz sighed. "He's not a creep, he's a well-known Morgan breeder, and one of his best mares was stolen a year ago."

A chill of recognition ran down Kate's spine. The last time Aunt Bea came to visit, she'd described the research she was doing on horse thieves. Her latest mystery novel was all about them.

"How can he prove it?" Holly said.

"Photos and registration papers," her mother said.

Head spinning, Kate collapsed on a tack trunk. This

was all happening to someone else, or it was a nightmare and she'd wake up in a minute and tell Holly and they'd laugh about it.

"I'm sorry, Kate," Liz said. "But try not to drive yourself nuts over this. There's always the chance that Tapestry isn't his horse. There are hundreds of other Morgans that look like her."

"What's he going to do?" Kate said, barely able to get the words out.

"He's coming to see her at the show."

"Then I'm not going," Kate said.

"Me neither," Holly said, defiantly. "Let Robin or Sue take my place."

"Don't be an idiot," Kate said. "You've got to go."

"Stop it, you two," Liz said. "If Mr. North doesn't see Tapestry at the show, he'll want to come here instead, and I intend to let him." Her voice softened. "Think about it, girls. If your horse were stolen, wouldn't you move heaven and earth to find her?"

"But she belongs to Kate," Holly wailed. "Didn't you tell him about the old man and the auction and that if Kate hadn't bought her she'd have been dog food?"

"Yes," Liz said, gently. "I told him everything, and he's very grateful. He wants to give Kate a reward. A *big* one."

Kate buried her face in her hands. "Please, Liz. Don't

say it. Don't say I can always buy another horse." She looked up with tears in her eyes. "Tapestry's the only one I want."

* * *

"It's my fault," Holly said, after they turned the horses out. "I shouldn't have posted those photos on Facebook."

"No, it's Angela's fault," Kate said.

Straddling the paddock fence, she watched Tapestry and Magician grazing nose-to-tail and swishing flies off each other's faces. The sun dappled Tapestry's copper-colored coat; her mane and tail shone like spun gold. Kate caught her breath. She'd never be able to replace her.

"Not this time," Holly said. "Mr. North can't have seen Angela's comments about Tapestry's collage unless he went to her page, and he can't do that unless he's a friend."

"Whatever," Kate said.

It made no difference how it happened. It just had, and she was stuck with it. But this was the last time she'd trust Facebook. First, it was Nathan's stupid fan page that caused trouble and now the barn's. From now on, she was sticking to e-mail and phone calls. Maybe her father was right: Native runners were slow, but they didn't spread vicious rumors on Facebook.

"I feel awful about this," Holly said. "I know exactly how you feel."

"How can you?" Kate said. "You've never lost a horse."

"Magician got stolen, remember?"

"Yeah, like he was gone for two whole days," Kate said. She hated herself for being snotty, but Holly's words had struck a nerve. "This isn't the same. I'm going to lose Tapestry, and—"

"No, you won't," Holly said. She banged the fence rail with her fist. "Tapestry isn't his horse. I can feel it in my bones."

But Kate didn't trust Holly's bones.

In a matter of days, she'd be saying goodbye to the one thing she loved most in the world, and there was nothing she could do about it.

Liz yelled from the barn. "Holly, it's your turn."

"In a minute," Holly yelled back. She turned to Kate. "I think Mom needs me to choose classes. Come and help me."

Kate shrugged. "Okay, but why?"

"Because I can't decide between junior jumping and gambler's choice."

"What's that?"

Holly grinned. "It's a bunch of jumps, and you take them in any order. That's the gamble. Do it fast, with the least faults, and you're the winner."

"Then Magician will clean up," Kate said.

Holly's horse was unbeatable when it came to tight turns and impossible angles. With a gulp, Kate imagined herself missing all this. No way could she let her best friend down.

She forced a smile. "Tell me about the apple-bobbing race."

"Does that mean you're coming to the show?" Holly said, looking hopeful.

Kate climbed off the fence. "I guess."

It was, in a way, her own gambler's choice. She'd taken a gamble on buying Tapestry, and now she had to take another by facing the guy who claimed to own her.

* * *

As the show loomed closer, so did Mrs. Dean's fancy dress party. Ideas flew around the barn faster than gossip on Facebook. One moment, Jennifer wanted to be a seahorse; the next, she changed her mind and was heavily into Zorro. Robin and Sue played it safe with Tonto and the Lone Ranger. Angela muttered something about unicorns.

"Sounds like a nightmare," Kate said.

"That's a good one," Holly said, writing it down. "Think of another."

Kate dug her toes in and declared she'd rather read a book on hoof ailments than make a fool of herself at the Timber Ridge clubhouse.

But Holly refused to give up.

She begged, cajoled, and threatened. Finally, she played her trump card. "You're a chicken, Kate McGregor, just like Tapestry and the stupid coop," she said. "You've got to face your worst fears."

With a jolt, Kate realized Holly was right, but she wasn't about to admit it. Most kids her age, especially boys, made her nervous. She had no experience hanging out with them. Well, except for Nathan, but he was ancient history.

"Oh, get a grip," she said. "This isn't a blind date."

"Close enough," Holly said. "Adam's bringing a friend, and he wants to meet you."

"Forget it," Kate said, but Holly dragged her into the basement anyway. She insisted on help with plowing through cartons of dress-up clothes and Halloween costumes. She held up one ridiculous outfit after another, making Kate laugh, until she finally gave in.

"Okay," Kate said. "All I need is a cape."

If she had to attend this dumb party, she'd stick to

her original idea—the headless horseman. She could hide beneath yards of cloth and not have to bother with makeup and hairdos and polishing her fingernails and talking to people who bored her witless.

Holly unearthed a wrinkled black cloak and shook it vigorously. Clouds of dust flew out. "This will do," she said, sneezing, She handed Kate a plastic Halloween pumpkin. "And here's your head."

"Does it have candy?" Kate said, peering inside.

"Dream on," Holly said. "I ate that years ago."

Rummaging further, she produced a skein of black yarn from her mother's knitting basket and draped it over the pumpkin. "Voilà. The headless horseman rides again. All that's missing is Ichabod Crane."

Kate gave a little gulp. "I'd rather have Nathan Crane."

"Oh, Kate, I'm sorry," Holly said, giving her a quick hug. "I bet there's a reason he hasn't written, or—"

"Like what?" Kate said. "He fell off the earth?"

"Maybe he's been sick, or they're shooting in caves again or on top of a mountain," Holly said, trying to untangle the yarn. "But Adam's buddy is cool. You'll like him."

"Does he ride?" Kate deadpanned.

Holly rolled her eyes. "You *always* ask that. If we were going to meet, oh, I dunno … someone's ninety-million-year-old grandmother, you'd want to know if she rode."

"If she's *that* old," Kate said, "she rode a woolly mammoth."

From a plastic storage box, Holly pulled a set of fairy wings, enormous black pipe cleaners, and a sparkly green cap that looked as if it once belonged to a pixie. She twisted the pipe cleaners into antennae and stuck them on her head. "What do you think?"

"You're a Martian?" Kate said.

Holly made a fashion adjustment. She poked holes in the pixie cap for her antennae, attached the fairy wings to her arms, and found a pair of oversized sunglasses that almost obliterated her face. "I'm a *horse*fly."

"Then you'll need ears, hooves, and a tail," Kate said.

"I've got a better idea." Holly climbed a stepladder and pulled a brown hobby-horse off the top shelf. It had a pink bridle.

"I never thought I'd ride *this* again," Holly said, cantering around the basement.

Kate grinned. "You still need a tail."

This was more fun than she was willing to admit. Maybe the dumb party wouldn't be so bad after all.

* * *

Early on Friday morning, Kate buckled Tapestry into a lungeing cavesson and led her into the outdoor ring. The barn was deserted, which suited Kate fine. Holly had offered to help, but Kate wanted to handle this on her own.

She tied Tapestry to the fence, fed her a carrot, and told her to pay attention as she laid a whole line of carrots on top of the chicken coop. For good measure, she scattered more on the ground in front of it. Tapestry eyed the treats eagerly.

"Not yet," Kate said. "You have to earn them."

Speaking softly, she walked Tapestry in big circles around the jump. "It's all about conquering fear," she told her horse. "If I can go to the silly costume party, then you can jump this silly wooden box."

Every few yards, she halted so Tapestry could look at the carrots. Kate plucked one off the ground. Tapestry whuffled it up and searched for more.

"Help yourself," Kate said.

She played out the lunge line. Tapestry stretched her nose toward the jump, snorted, and leaped back. Immediately, Kate led her away, then realized she wasn't alone. Leaning on the fence, less than fifteen feet away, were Angela and Courtney.

"Taking your little can of doggie food for a walk?" Courtney said, loud enough for Kate to hear.

"No, she's wasting her time," drawled Angela. "That horse will never jump the coop. She's scared, just like her rider. I bet she's too scared to come to my mother's party tonight." There was a pause. "Did you know she's got a crush on Nathan Crane?"

"The *actor*?" Courtney said, in mock surprise.

"None other," Angela said, as if they were following a well-rehearsed script. "Nathan's in the *Moonlight* movie. You know, the one where Kate McGregor stole the part from me? She threw herself all over him, and he got so freaked out that he asked me for my cell number."

"Did you give it to him?" Courtney asked.

Angela grinned. "What do you think?"

"Wow," Courtney said, sounding impressed, like she'd never heard it all before.

"We hang out on Facebook all the time," Angela said. "Me and Nathan Crane ... we're really close, like this." She held up her arms and crossed them.

Courtney gave her cousin a high five.

Kate did her best to ignore them. Trading insults with Angela and Courtney was like fighting a barn fire with squirt guns. But what if Angela wasn't just showing off? Suppose Nathan really *had* been in touch with her? That would explain his silence.

Gritting her teeth, Kate concentrated on Tapestry. If she spun this out long enough, Angela and Courtney would get bored and disappear. She led Tapestry away from the coop and into another circle. Now and then, she fed her a small carrot, just to keep her interest up and remind her that they really did have a job to do.

"Don't you have a lesson to prepare for?"

His voice took Kate by surprise. For a moment, she thought it was directed at her. But the trainer was glowering at Angela, who seemed to be shrinking into herself. She said something to him that Kate couldn't hear, then grabbed her cousin's hand and fled into the barn.

Vincent King ducked under the fence and strode toward Kate. "That's not the right way to do it," he said, tapping his boots with a bamboo cane. He reached for Tapestry's lunge line. "Let me show you."

"No, thank you," Kate said. "We're doing fine."

"You'll never get her over that jump with carrots. You need to teach her who's boss." The trainer held up his crop. "This always works," he said. "Here, take it. I've got plenty more."

Kate curled her fist around the knotted bamboo. It bit into her flesh, and she was tempted to break the vicious weapon into pieces. Instead, she thrust it back at him.

"I don't like whips," she said.

Vincent King shot her an icy glare, then turned around and strode off. At his heels, something glinted and Kate realized he was wearing spurs. They had tiny rowels in them.

She shuddered and coiled up her lunge line. Maybe they'd done enough for one day. But Tapestry had other ideas. She gave Kate a nudge that nearly sent her flying and dragged her toward the coop. She snatched a carrot from the ground, crunched it down, and vacuumed up all the others.

Kate wiped dirt off her mare's whiskers. "Way to go, girl."

She was about to lead her away when Tapestry surprised her again. She snatched a carrot off the coop, then another, and Kate stared open-mouthed as her horse gobbled up the entire row.

The last carrot fell behind the jump.

Tapestry leaned over and looked at it, tantalizingly out of reach. Then, before Kate could stop her, she hopped nimbly over the coop and claimed her last treat.

11

"HOLD STILL," HOLLY SAID. "You're driving me nuts." She wiped a blob of mascara off Kate's cheek. "Open your eyes wider, and don't blink."

Staring straight ahead, Kate obeyed.

This had been going on for half an hour, and Kate was still shocked at how smoothly Holly had talked her into a makeover. One minute she'd been washing her face and dragging a brush through her wet hair; the next, Holly was comparing her with Tapestry.

"If your horse can jump the coop, you can put up with a little eye shadow," Holly announced, while applying her own. "You can't hide under that stupid cloak all evening. You'll be hotter than a microwaved pudding in there."

Not only that, Kate now realized, but she'd be uncomfortable as well. They'd borrowed two sets of football pads from Sue's brother to bump up her shoulders. Holly said she looked like a deformed linebacker, but Kate had to take her word for it because Holly had covered their bedroom mirror with a beach towel.

"No peeking," Holly said.

Littered across the dresser, Kate counted nine shades of eye shadow, five lip pencils, seven tubes of gloss, and a forest of makeup brushes jammed into a plastic mug with Magician's photo on the front. Somehow, Holly had managed to use them all.

"Ta-dah," she finally said and unveiled the mirror with a flourish. "What do you think?"

Kate stared at her reflection.

A glamorous stranger stared back.

"You look like Emma Watson," Holly said, tucking Kate's hair behind her ears.

Kate leaned closer. Her eyes sparkled, her cheeks glowed, and those two zits she'd obsessed over that morning had totally disappeared. Even her lips looked shiny and new.

"I love it," she breathed.

"*Told* you," Holly said, grinning.

* * *

The party was in full swing by the time they got there. Liz, looking cool and elegant in her old dressage outfit, joined Angela's mother and Vincent King at the buffet table. A black feather boa hung from Mrs. Dean's scrawny neck, and she kept adjusting the straps of her red satin gown. It was so tight, she could barely walk.

"What's she supposed to be?" Kate whispered from beneath her voluminous cape. They'd cut a slit for her eyes and covered it with mesh from a broken window screen. She could see just fine as long as she didn't move her head and lose the opening.

"A clothes horse?" Jennifer said.

Holly snorted. "More like a charley horse."

A pair of My Little Ponies trotted by. They wore hot pink bell boots, rainbow wigs with perky blue ears, and more eye makeup than Lady Gaga. Holly gave a little neigh and cantered up to them on her hobby horse.

"Hey, Angela," she said. "One of your false eyelashes fell off. I thought it was a spider, so I stomped on it."

The DJ drowned Angela's reply. Drums and guitars exploded through the loudspeakers with Justin Bieber at full throttle. The Lone Ranger and Tonto invited Kate to dance. She tried a few steps, trod on her cloak, and gave up. There was an itch somewhere beneath her shoulder pads.

Holly buzzed past, flapping her wings. "Adam's here."

"Where?" Kate said.

"Coming through the door." Holly whipped off her sunglasses. "Oops, I think he's stuck."

Strobes flashed, and a disco ball spun overhead, fragmenting the dance floor into a million tiny lights. Kate felt dizzy. She wanted to rub her eyes, but couldn't get at them through the folds of her cloak. Adam wobbled into her line of sight. He appeared to have four legs.

"He's a cart horse?" Kate said.

Holly squealed. "No, he's a centaur."

Jockeys and cowboys scattered as Adam lumbered toward them. He wore a leather vest, Viking horns, and baggy pants cobbled together from feed bags. They hung low on his hips, held up with baling twine suspenders.

"I feel sorry for his buddy," Holly whispered.

"Me, too," Kate said. The poor guy was bent double, hanging onto Adam's waist, and covered from head to toe in itchy grain sacks. Across his back were the words *Purina Horse Chow*.

"Awesome costume," Holly said and planted a kiss on Adam's cheek.

He blushed. "I made it myself."

"Yeah, right," came a muffled voice behind him. "But I'm doing all the hard work."

The DJ cranked up his sound system and left Kate's ears ringing. Oh, great. Now she was deaf as well as half blind and bakingly hot.

* * *

An hour later, Kate decided she'd had enough. Sweat trickled down her back; the itch on her right shoulder had taken on a life of its own. "I'm going," she told Holly.

Her eyes widened. "Home?"

"No," Kate said. "To the ladies' room."

Once inside, Kate ripped off her cloak, unbuckled the football pads, and sank into an overstuffed chair. Even her eyebrows were exhausted. Being a headless horseman was hard work. Wearily, she examined her makeup —not as bad as she expected—and finger combed her hair. Did she really look like Emma Watson?

Holly had to be dreaming.

Feeling a whole lot more comfortable in jeans and a t-shirt, Kate stuffed her costume behind the chair and rejoined the others. Adam's front end was still bopping with Holly, but his hindquarters kept tripping over his cardboard hooves. Any minute now, there'd be a major pileup on the dance floor.

Mrs. Dean clapped her hands. It was time for the prizes, and Mr. King had kindly agreed to give them out.

The DJ produced a suitable drum roll. Eyes turned toward the podium, and before Mrs. Dean had time to announce the winner of prettiest costume, up trotted the two My Little Ponies to collect their matching blue ribbons.

"Are we surprised?" Holly said.

Jennifer adjusted her Zorro mask, then made a sweeping Z sign with her sword that sent the Lone Ranger's hat flying. Tonto was told to go and get it, but Tonto shrugged and said, "Get it yourself, kemosabe."

Kate gave Tonto a high five.

After more awards for weirdest, scariest, and most original costumes, Adam snagged first prize for funniest. He performed a clumsy piaffe and bowed like a circus pony. Everyone laughed, except for Vincent King who didn't even crack a smile.

"I've seen him before," Adam said.

"Where?"

"A show, maybe. Or a magazine." He shrugged. "I'm starving. I could eat a horse."

A muffled neigh came from his hindquarters.

* * *

Loaded up with miniburgers, cupcakes, and bottles of soda, they decamped to a picnic table on the patio. Trees and umbrellas sparkled with fairy lights; the swimming pool beckoned.

Kate wanted to jump in.

"Okay, buddy," Adam said, thumping his hindquarters. "You'd better come out because I need to sit down."

There was much shuffling as Adam's other half extricated himself from a complicated arrangement of grain sacks and baling twine. With a loud groan, he stood up and stretched. A hank of streaky blond hair fell across his forehead; his green eyes locked onto Kate's.

"Nathan?" she said.

Holly grinned and flung her arms around him.

"Yikes," he said, holding onto his back. "I may never stand up straight again."

Questions zoomed through Kate's head: *What was Nathan doing here and why hadn't he warned her? Why hadn't Adam? Did Holly know he was coming?* Kate sat down hard on the picnic bench and wished she was still inside her cloak. That way, if she needed to cry, nobody would know.

* * *

It took Nathan less than five minutes to explain. He'd caught a weird bug the doctors couldn't identify, and they confined him to the isolation unit of a hospital in Bucharest.

To make matters even worse, his cell phone went

missing, and the studio refused to replace it. They didn't want news about his illness going public. It might harm the movie or Nathan's image. Only his family was told what had happened. His fans had no idea. He wasn't allowed to contact anyone except his parents in California.

"Are you okay now?" Kate said. He looked healthy enough. He even had a tan.

"Yeah, I'm fine," Nathan said. "It turned out to be nothing serious, but the tests took weeks to come back. I honestly thought I'd be stuck in that place forever." He slid onto the bench beside her. "I had no way of calling you, until yesterday when I landed in New York. But then I chickened out, and—"

"Called me instead," Holly said.

Kate sucked in her breath. "Why?"

"Because I wasn't sure you'd even talk to me," Nathan said. "I figured you'd be mad at me for"—he hesitated—"all those dumb rumors."

"What rumors?" Kate said.

Nathan blushed. "About me and my co-star."

"Tess O'Donnell?" Kate said.

She was blonde and drop-dead gorgeous and one of Holly's favorite stars. She was also one of the nicest girls Kate had ever met. They'd worked together on the movie, with Kate riding as a stunt-double for Tess.

"Yeah." Nathan's blush grew deeper. "The fan mags have us about ready to elope."

"Way to go, dude," Adam said. "I'll loan you a ladder."

"Not funny," Holly said, and smacked him. "Those rumors are gross. You know they're not true."

"So, are you and me, like, okay?" Nathan said, squeezing Kate's hand and letting it go. "I mean, you're not mad at me, or anything?"

He was like a puppy, caught in the act of chewing someone's slippers. Kate didn't know whether to laugh or cry. Instead, she decided to play it cool. Let him suffer … just for a few seconds.

"No, I'm not mad," she said, trying to keep a straight face. "Well, only a little bit."

"What about?" He looked genuinely puzzled.

She plucked at the grain sack still wrapped around his shoulders. "Why did you hide behind Adam all night?"

He grinned at her. "Why did you hide inside that cloak?"

"Touché," Holly said.

"I asked first," Kate said, not taking her eyes off Nathan.

"Blame your best friend," he said, looking sheepish. "It was her idea."

"That's because I wanted to surprise you," Holly said. "I thought it would be fun. Besides, I had to figure out a disguise for Nathan. The girls would've mobbed him if Adam hadn't kept him hidden."

Kate put a hand to her face. No wonder Holly had insisted on a makeover. She knew Nathan was coming to the party because she'd organized it. She probably knew about the stupid rumors, as well. She read all the fan sites and magazines, yet she hadn't said a word, knowing Kate would be upset.

At that moment, the patio door slid open. Vincent King stepped out, lit a cigarette, and walked past the picnic table without appearing to notice anyone was there. For a brief moment, his face caught the light.

Adam let out a low whistle. "I've got it."

"Got what?" Kate said.

"That guy, Angela's trainer. I saw it on YouTube. His horse refused a fence—it was a big, international competition— and he went ballistic. He hauled off and beat the horse, like ten times, and the judges suspended him."

Holly said, "Then I bet you anything his name isn't Vincent King."

Adam reached for his cell phone, punched a few buttons, and whistled again. "It's Victor Kavanaugh."

Kate gasped. "He was on the British show-jumping team. They won the World Cup three years ago."

"Yeah," Adam said. "And nobody's seen him since then."

In a flash, Kate glued the pieces together—Vincent King's bamboo crop, his assistant's mysterious bag, Angela's erratic behavior, and now this. It all fell into place.

Quickly, she filled the others in.

"Okay, Nancy Drew," Holly said. "So what should we do about it?"

"Tell your mom?" Nathan said. "Or Angela's?"

"No proof," Adam said. "You can't accuse people without solid evidence."

"So how do we get it?" Holly said.

Kate thought for a minute. "One of us has to sneak into the indoor arena and watch Angela's lesson."

"When?"

"Tomorrow," Kate said. "Her trainer's coming at noon."

12

When Nathan arrived the next morning, Kate barely recognized him. A dark brown wig covered his streaky blond hair, and he peered at her owlishly through wire-rimmed glasses. On his chin, he sported a straggly goatee. Holly gave it a little tug.

"Ouch," he said. "You're pulling it off."

"So, what's with the disguise?" Kate said.

"To fool the fans," Adam said, in a stage whisper. "We don't want him to get mobbed." He nudged his buddy. "We're calling him Tom Smith today, if anyone asks."

"Well, that's his real name, anyway," Kate said.

That's how he'd introduced himself the first time they met. Later Kate had found out he was also Nathan Crane, and Holly teased her for not recognizing him.

"Okay," Adam said. "What's the plan?"

Holly laid it out. She and Nathan would stand guard in the barn while Adam and Kate spied on Angela from a storage closet in the arena's observation room. They would set their cell phones to vibrate and Holly would text Kate the minute Vincent King arrived. Whatever photos and videos Adam managed to get, he would send immediately to Nathan's iPhone.

"Very cloak-and-dagger," Adam said.

Nathan grinned. "Like a James Bond movie."

"We'd better get going," Kate said. "It's eleven-thirty, and Vincent King is never late."

Nobody else was around. Liz had taken a group of students to jump the hunt course, so they'd be gone for at least an hour. Angela wouldn't show up till noon, but her little sister, Marcia, would be along at any minute to groom Skywalker. Nathan wanted to see Kate's horse before she and Adam went into hiding.

"Okay," Kate said. "But we've got to make it quick."

She led him to Tapestry's stall. The mare whickered and stuck her nose out for carrots. "Sorry girl," Kate said, patting her. "You ate them all yesterday."

"She's movie-star gorgeous," Nathan said. "It's kinda hard to believe you rescued her from an auction. Do you ever wonder who used to own her?"

"All the time," Kate said. "I'll tell you about it later."

Softly, he said, "Be careful in there. Holly and I will be right outside the door. We'll be with you in a flash if you need us."

Kate gulped. This was getting scarier by the minute.

* * *

The closet was stuffed with equipment. Adam and Kate moved jump stands and folding chairs to make room for themselves. Adam shut the door. It had a dirty window up high. Adam was tall enough to peer through it, but Kate had to climb on a box. Adam found a rag and cleaned the glass. Two spiders scuttled out of sight.

"That's better," he said. "Now we can see."

They had a clear view of the arena and all the jumps—the wall, the brush jump, and a medley of oxers and crossrails made from PVC pipes which Liz liked because they were lightweight and easy to move around.

Kate's cell phone vibrated. *VK here.*

Angela? Kate texted back.

Not yet.

Moments later, the arena doors slid open and Vincent King strode inside, followed by his assistant. While he adjusted jumps, Sharon pulled on a pair of gloves, grabbed a PVC pole, and wrapped it with wire. Then she did something Kate couldn't see because the double oxer blocked her vision.

Kate's cell phone buzzed again.

Heads up, Holly texted. *Angela*.

Nostrils flaring, Skywalker burst through the doors. His ears were pinned; his mahogany coat glistened with sweat. Gobs of foam flew from his mouth and spattered onto his shoulders like miniature marshmallows.

For the next ten minutes, Angela trotted and cantered her fractious horse in circles. Her hands were rigid, and her back was as stiff as the bamboo cane she carried. Kate recognized it immediately. Vincent King had another, sticking up from his left boot. As if that wasn't enough, he also held a dressage whip with tassels on the end. He gave Angela a curt nod. She popped over the brush jump, barely cleared the double oxer, and sent the parallel bars flying.

Kate flinched.

"Ouch," Adam whispered.

Angela's trainer snapped his whip. "Sloppy work," he yelled. "Do it over, and do it right this time."

Tucking the dressage whip beneath his arm, he pulled on the second pair of rubber gloves and nodded to his assistant—some sort of secret code. They positioned themselves on each side of the crossrail, which now had a pole on top—the same one Sharon had wrapped with wire.

On a tight rein, Angela cantered past the observation

room, unaware that Adam was videotaping her. She turned and headed for the crossrail. The moment her horse took off, Vincent King and Sharon raised the top pole, and Skywalker's forelegs rapped it.

"They're poling him," Adam said, still shooting.

Kate gasped. "But that's illegal."

She'd never seen it done before, but she'd certainly heard about it. Some unscrupulous trainers even used poles with spikes and carpet tacks in them—whatever it took to inflict enough pain so the horse would remember to pick its legs up. Kate stared at the crossrail's PVC pipe. It had clips at each end, with more wires attached to the plastic box she'd seen in Sharon's bag.

"What *is* that?" she said, pointing.

Adam said, "It looks like a portable fence charger."

"You mean, they're *zapping* him, too?"

Angela's horse thundered toward the jump again. Up went the pole, but this time, Skywalker cleared it with a foot to spare.

"I guess that's the general idea," Adam said. "But it's not working because Vincent King and Sharon obviously failed eighth-grade physics."

"They did?" Kate said, puzzled.

"Think about birds on a power line," Adam said, snapping off another photo. "They're sitting on a gazillion volts of electricity, but they don't get fried."

Kate cringed as Skywalker took the jump again. "Okay, I kind of get that," she said. "But why?"

"Because the birds aren't grounded," Adam said. "You need a complete circuit to conduct electricity. When Angela's horse touches the wire, all his feet are off the ground, so—"

"He's like a bird?"

"Exactly," Adam said. "The only thing he feels is the pole rapping his legs."

"So why are Vincent King and Sharon wearing gloves?"

"Because they're standing on the ground," Adam said. "The gloves help to protect them if they touch the wire and get zapped."

"Like when you touch an electric fence," Kate said.

There was an electric fence around the back paddock, but Liz only turned it on at night. Kate had touched the wire once and gotten a serious tingle. No wonder the horses never went near it.

Adam nodded, as Angela careened toward the jump again. But this time her horse dug in his toes. Swerving to the left, he skidded past Vincent King, almost knocking him over. The trainer whacked Skywalker with his whip, then raised it for another blow.

"No," Kate screamed. "No!"

She shoved Adam to one side. He crashed into a

stack of chairs as Kate opened the door and zoomed out of the closet. This was crazy, but she couldn't stop herself. Heart pounding, she raced across the tanbark toward Vincent King. For a frozen moment, he just stood there, as if unable to believe his eyes.

"Kate," Adam yelled. "Stop!"

Kate heard him charging up behind her, but she wanted revenge. She lunged forward and snatched the whip from Vincent King's hand. In a flash, he grabbed her wrist and squeezed it so hard, she dropped the whip. Without letting go of Kate, he pulled the cane from his boot.

"You stupid, silly girl," he snarled. "You'll pay for this."

His arm flew up, ready to smash her. Kate twisted and kicked. She tried to remember the judo lessons she'd taken in third grade. *Keep moving. Don't give him a target.* Jerking her head to one side, she saw Angela and Skywalker, bearing down on them like a valkyrie.

Just in time, Adam yanked her out of the way.

Vincent King staggered backward, right into Skywalker's path, and Kate watched—open mouthed—as Angela leaned forward and whacked her trainer in the face with his own bamboo cane. He screamed and doubled over.

Kate felt herself go limp. This time she really was going to faint.

* * *

By the time Kate opened her eyes, Holly was crouched beside her. Ten feet away, Adam and Nathan had Vincent King by both arms. A livid red mark ran across his forehead, and blood trickled from his nose. There was no sign of Angela and Skywalker.

"Are you all right?" Holly said, looking anxious.

"I think so." Kate struggled to her feet. "Where's Sharon?" Her rubber gloves were lying beside the cross-rail.

"Gone," Holly said. "But she won't get far."

"Why not?"

Holly held up a set of keys. "Nathan removed these from VK's truck."

Just then, Liz sprinted toward them. Kate heaved a sigh of relief. This situation had gotten seriously out of hand. It needed a grownup to fix it. After making sure the kids were okay, Liz turned on Vincent King.

"I've got a hysterical girl in my barn, along with a freaked-out horse that's covered in sweat," she said, glaring at him. "Would you care to explain?"

He shook himself free of Adam and Nathan, then made a big show of wiping blood from his nose. "It's none of your business," he snapped. "Mrs. Dean hired me to coach her daughter, not you."

"Sounds more like abuse to me," Liz said.

Taking turns, Adam and Kate gave her the rundown.

The trainer stiffened. "It's my word against theirs. You can't prove anything."

"Oh, yes we can," Adam said, holding up his iPhone.

Vincent King snatched the phone. He threw it on the ground and stomped on it. The glass shattered.

"Too late," Adam said. "I already sent the videos to YouTube." He pinned Angela's trainer with a look. "And you owe me two hundred bucks for a new cell phone."

Kate shuddered. This whole fiasco was Mrs. Dean's fault and all because of a local horse show. She wanted Angela to win blue ribbons so badly that she didn't even care if the trainer she hired to do the job used threats and a cattle prod.

* * *

After kicking Vincent King out, Liz called Mrs. Dean and gave her an earful. She told her in no uncertain terms to fire Angela's trainer.

"Will he go to jail?" Holly said.

Her mother sighed. "At worst, he'll get a fine, but only if someone prosecutes, and I doubt Mrs. Dean will."

"But that's not fair," Holly protested. "He's a bad

135

guy. He needs to be punished. Look at all the horses he's hurt."

"And riders," Kate murmured.

She couldn't take her mind off Angela's terrified face as she laid into Vincent King with the bamboo cane. Kate had found it lying in the tanbark. She'd picked it up, snapped it over her knee, and dumped the pieces in a trash bin.

Robin and Sue had already taken care of Skywalker. They'd sponged him down and cooled him out in the back paddock. Angela, still in tears, was wrapped in a blanket in Liz's office. Nathan and Adam drove her home, then continued on to Adam's house. They had to get his horse ready for Monday's show. It was being held at Larchwood Stables—Timber Ridge's biggest rival— and Adam was its star rider.

Liz's cell phone rang. She answered, nodded a couple of times, and hung up.

"Angela's dropped out of the show."

13

LIZ CANCELED THE RIDING TEAM'S AFTERNOON LESSON. There'd been enough trauma for one day. They would practice in the morning, and Kate would get another chance to coax Tapestry over the coop—under saddle, this time. Afterward, there'd be a team picnic at the lake. But right now, they had horses to groom and tack to clean.

"This is so cool," Holly said, buffing her stirrups. "You're on the team. Aren't you glad?"

"Yes, no ... I don't know," Kate said.

Holly grinned. "Make up your mind."

Forcing a smile, Kate rubbed soap into her bridle. On Monday, Tapestry would wear her sparkly new brow-band for the first time. It might also be the last. Kate swallowed hard. Her guts were in turmoil. Half of her was ecstatic about being on the team with Holly; the other half was in a total panic over the mysterious Richard North. Then there was her idiotic compulsion to beat Angela Dean. Somehow, it had gone crazily wrong.

All she'd wanted was a chance to compete against Angela on equal terms—and on her own horse. But it hadn't worked out that way, and now she'd just been handed the booby prize because Angela had dropped out.

Kate knew it wasn't her fault, but all the same she felt guilty. If she hadn't attacked Vincent King, maybe Angela wouldn't have gone ballistic.

Holly told her she was nuts.

"Angela was a time bomb waiting to explode," she said. "It's her mother's fault. She hired a crooked trainer, and Angela got caught in the crossfire. You know what she's been like, with the crying and stuff. Well, today, she finally lost it."

"I don't blame her," Kate said.

Holly shivered. "Me neither."

They were silent for a moment. Then Kate said, "Maybe one of us should, like, go and see if she's okay."

"You mean walk into the lion's den?" Holly said.

Kate had never been to the Deans' house. "Yeah."

"Better not," Holly said. "She'd throw us out."

* * *

After dinner, Kate wandered back to the barn. Holly was in their bedroom, trying on outfits for school. It would start on Wednesday. Kate couldn't think that far ahead, not when there was Monday to get through first.

She fed Tapestry half a bag of carrots and shared the rest between Magician and Skywalker. He seemed none the worse for his dramatic afternoon.

But what about Angela? Was she utterly miserable?

Kate knew the feeling. At her old stables, she'd been blamed for the death of a valuable show jumper. It wasn't her fault, but it had taken ages for the truth to come out. Kate had suffered months of misery and self-doubt. In fact, she'd sworn off horses forever ... until she came to live at Timber Ridge with Holly and Liz.

Angela wasn't in the same boat, but misery was misery, no matter the cause. She was probably scared and lonely, and Kate was willing to bet Courtney had already abandoned her and gone off to play tennis.

It wouldn't hurt to look around.

As Kate drew closer to the Timber Ridge club house, she could hear voices and laughter. Music drifted out. Lights shone on the tennis courts, and a girl with long, blond hair jumped into the swimming pool.

Kate hid behind a bush.

Courtney surfaced and swam to the edge. Kate looked around for Angela. Maybe she was inside.

Clutching a martini glass, Mrs. Dean tottered across the patio.

"Come along, dear," she said to her niece. "Dinner's ready. Your uncle and I are waiting."

No mention of Angela. Had she been grounded for defying her mother's precious trainer?

* * *

A long, sweeping driveway led to the Deans' three-story house. Its front entrance had a portico supported by columns. It reminded Kate of the White House. On each side of the door sat two stone lions, like the ones at the New York Public Library, only a bit smaller.

Kate reached for the door knocker—a brass lion's head—and changed her mind. She pressed the bell instead. Almost immediately, the door opened, as if whoever had been standing behind it had seen her coming up the driveway and was waiting.

Marcia's head peeked out.

"Hi," Kate said. "Is, um, is Angela around?"

Marcia's eyes opened wider. So did the door. Beyond it, Kate had a glimpse of gilt statues and massive flower arrangements. On the black-and-red tile floor lay a shaggy white rug.

"Who's there?" came a familiar voice.

Kate stiffened. Maybe this wasn't such a great idea,

after all. She turned to leave, but Angela stepped outside.

"Did you come to gloat?" she said.

Her eyes were puffy, her face red and blotchy, and her hair looked as if it hadn't been washed in a month.

"No," Kate said. "I wanted to see if—"

"What?"

"Are you okay?" Kate said.

Angela snorted. "Do I look okay?"

Behind her, the door snapped shut. Angela gave a shuddering sigh and climbed onto one of the lions. Kate straddled the other one. It felt cold and scratchy beneath her bare legs.

"I used to ride these when I was a kid," Angela said.

Taken by surprise, Kate said, "I had a rocking horse."

"What color was it?"

"Pink and white," Kate said, "with a silver mane and tail."

"I had one of those, too." Angela let out another sigh. "My sister still rides it when she thinks nobody is looking."

This was an insane conversation, but at least they were talking. Kate said, "Look, I don't want to know what happened, you know, afterward, but I—" She gulped. "I'm sorry, and I feel really bad."

Angela made a choking sound.

Now what? Stick around, or get off the lion and leave? Kate had no idea. Her cell phone buzzed.

Where are you? Holly had texted.

Kate turned it off.

"We're having a team picnic tomorrow," she said, not daring to look at Angela. "Come with us."

* * *

The final team practice went without a hitch. Tapestry jumped the chicken coop like it was no big deal, Jennifer and Rebel performed a flawless equitation routine, and Holly rode Magician over the jump course so fast it made Kate's head spin.

"Do that tomorrow, and you've got gambler's choice in the bag," she said, as they cooled off their horses.

"Fat chance," Holly said. "Adam's in it."

"Then don't you dare let him win," Kate warned. A girl at her old school who was totally brilliant at math and science had deliberately scored low on her finals so her less-than-brilliant boyfriend wouldn't feel bad.

Holly snorted. "As if I would."

Riding bareback, Sue and Robin jogged by. They wore bathing suits, muck boots, and crash helmets. Liz told the others to hurry up. She would pack the truck and meet them at the lake. Sue's dad was bringing his barbecue grill, and Robin's mother had made the kids' favorite sheet cake. There would be watermelon and s'mores. Jennifer's parents had promised plenty of soda.

"Do you think Angela will come?" Holly said.

Kate shrugged. "I dunno."

"But you did invite her, right?"

"Yeah," Kate said.

Holly rolled her eyes as if she still couldn't quite believe Kate had actually gone to see Angela. At this point, Kate could hardly believe it herself. What *had* she been thinking? Angela had brushed off her invitation with an icy stare and stomped back inside the house.

Leaving their horses in the barn, they raced home to change. Kate couldn't find her bathing suit, so she borrowed a black tankini from Holly and threw on a pair of faded old jeans she'd cut off at the knees. She grabbed a beach towel, then realized she had no idea how Tapestry felt about water.

"She'll be fine," Holly said. "She'll follow Magician anywhere, and you know he's a water baby."

* * *

Holly was right. Kate had no sooner ridden Tapestry into the lake than her knees buckled, her hindquarters collapsed, and Kate found herself swimming. Sue and Robin rode their horses in to join her, then Holly and

Magician splashed alongside. The only holdout was Rebel. For all his macho behavior, he flatly refused to go anywhere near the water.

After their picnic, Kate left her friends hanging out on the beach and took Tapestry for a walk. This might be their last chance to be alone together. She sat on a rock with her feet in the water and watched Tapestry paddle. How much longer would she own her?

Quietly, she began to cry.

14

NATHAN CALLED AT SIX-THIRTY the next morning when Kate was braiding Tapestry's mane. It was taking ten times longer than normal because there was so much of it.

"I'm sorry," he said. "But I'm gonna miss your show."

Kate's heart sank. Even though Nathan knew nothing about horses, he'd spent Sunday helping Adam get ready and declared he would cheer for Larchwood as well as for Timber Ridge.

"No favorites," he'd promised.

But the studio's travel center had changed Nathan's flight. He was leaving for California today, not tomorrow as planned, and then flying on to New Zealand where the rest of the filming would take place.

Even further away than Romania.

Kate bit her lip. She would *not* cry. Whatever tears she had left were saved for Tapestry. She would not waste them on a guy, even if he was devastatingly cute.

"Bummer," Holly said and gave her a hug. She lowered her voice. "Don't look now, but Marcia's grooming Skywalker."

"Why?" Kate said. "Angela's not riding."

"Maybe somebody forgot to tell her little sister," Holly said.

The other girls showed up. They got busy brushing their horses, and in no time, the barn was buzzing with nerves and excitement.

"I'm gonna knock down all the jumps," Sue moaned.

Robin sighed. "Me, too."

"Rebel's in a bad mood," said Jennifer. "He'll flub up the trail class for sure."

Liz told the kids to hustle. They would be leaving in half an hour.

* * *

Larchwood Equestrian Center was a forty-minute drive from Timber Ridge, and Holly spent most of it texting with Adam. He'd gotten a new cell phone. Kate glanced at hers.

Good luck, Nathan had texted. *Miss you.*

She thought about all the girls in the world who'd kill for a text from Nathan Crane and felt warm inside. It helped take her mind off Tapestry's uncertain future … at least for a few minutes.

Liz parked the van beneath a large maple. She told the girls to unload their horses and then disappeared to get exhibitor numbers and coffee. Kate was leading Tapestry down the ramp when a familiar car caught her eye—Mrs. Dean's silver Mercedes. So, she'd come to the show after all.

"I bet she's madder than a wet hen," Holly said.

Kate tied Tapestry to the van. "Why?"

"This is her biggest charity, remember?" Holly said. "She probably invited all her fancy friends to watch Angela win ribbons, but now she's doing damage control because Angela isn't here."

Looking around, Kate realized this was a really big event, bigger than a county fair. The parking lot was crammed with horse trailers from all over New England. In the distance rose a giant Ferris wheel and the pagoda roof of a carousel. Maybe she and Holly would get to ride them later.

Just then, Adam trotted up on Domino, his half-Arabian pinto. "Have you heard the news?"

"About Nathan?" Kate said. "He called this morning, and—"

Maggie Dana

"No," Adam said, jumping off his horse. "About Angela."

Holly groaned. "What has she done now?"

"She's joined the Larchwood team."

There was a stunned silence. Then Holly said, "You have *got* to be kidding."

Adam shook his head. "Nope."

"The rotten little traitor," Holly said. "Whose place did she steal?"

"Nobody's," Adam said. "We lost a rider last night. Her horse pulled up lame."

"So what classes is Angela in?" Kate said.

"Equitation and junior show jumping," Adam said. He patted Domino's neck. "I'm not in either one."

"But we are," Holly said.

Kate sucked in her breath. *Finally*, she'd get to compete against Angela on equal terms *and* on her own horse. A few moments later, Liz confirmed it. One of the Larchwood grooms had just delivered Skywalker to the show grounds.

"No wonder Marcia was grooming him," Holly said.

* * *

Holly's equitation class was so big that the judges split it into two groups with separate prizes for each. Jennifer's group rode first, and she captured second place. Liz hung her red ribbon on the van's windshield.

"Well done," she said, looking pleased.

Kate crossed her fingers as Holly entered the ring, three horses behind Angela. "Good luck," she said. "You've gotta beat her, okay?"

"I will, don't worry," Holly said.

Leaning on the rail, Kate almost forgot about the cloud hanging over her head. Magician looked superb. He trotted and cantered without putting a foot wrong. Holly sat tall and straight in the saddle, in perfect command of her horse. Nobody would ever guess she'd been stuck in a wheelchair for the past two years.

The judge told the competitors to line up. Holly was too far away for Kate to see her face clearly, but she could imagine what her best friend was feeling—nervous and excited and determined to win.

One by one, each rider performed a figure eight, then trotted in a straight line toward the judge. Angela's figure eight was sloppy, and when she rode down the centerline, her toes stuck out at right angles.

Holly's figure eight was flawless.

The officials conferred, and Kate held her breath. No way could Angela win this class, but if she did, it would mean her mother had bribed the judge. After an interminable wait, the sixth-place winner was announced, followed by fifth and fourth. Angela placed third and accepted her yellow ribbon with a scowl. Second place went to a rider from Spruce Hill Farm.

"And the winner is—"

Liz grabbed Kate's arm. Robin and Sue covered their eyes. Jennifer crossed her fingers.

"—Holly Chapman, of Timber Ridge."

"Whoo-hoo!" Kate cried, and punched the air with her fist as the judge pinned a blue ribbon to Magician's bridle. Blue looked perfect on a black horse, never mind that Holly said it was better on chestnuts. The winners made a victory lap. As they cantered by, Angela's face was dark as thunder; Holly's smile was a ray of sunshine.

After hugging her ecstatic daughter, Liz turned to Kate and told her to saddle up. "The pleasure class starts in ten minutes."

Liz's words brought Kate back down to earth. She looked around for anyone who might be Richard North, but so far nobody seemed to fit the bill. No strange man had snooped around the Timber Ridge van or asked questions about their horses. Maybe, just maybe, he'd changed his mind and decided Tapestry wasn't his after all.

Kate hung onto that thought as she got ready for her class. It was almost as big as Holly's but the judge didn't split it this time. The other horses looked so sleek and gorgeous that Kate didn't think she stood much of a chance.

Liz patted her boot. "Don't forget to smile."

Kate didn't feel much like smiling. There were a dozen men scattered around the rail, observing her class. More were up in the bleachers. Any one of them could be Richard North. A tall guy wearing tan jodhpurs and a denim vest tipped his baseball cap as she trotted by. Was that him?

To distract herself, Kate ran through her mental checklist: *Pick up the right diagonal, don't canter on the wrong lead, never cut corners, and keep well away from the other riders.* She plastered a smile on her face and hoped it didn't look too much like a grimace.

After the competitors trotted and cantered in both directions, the ring steward called out six numbers. To Kate's surprise, hers was one of them. She lined up with the other finalists, then glanced toward her cheering section. Liz waved. Holly and Adam gave her a thumbs-up.

There was no sign of the guy in tan jodhpurs.

Tapestry breezed through their individual workout. Ears pricked, she cantered a perfect circle, trotted in a straight line, and backed up the required four steps without making a fuss. Kate patted her neck.

"Good girl," she whispered.

Finally, the results were called. Larchwood took the blue ribbon, with Spruce Hill in second place, and Kate in third. She wanted to cheer and throw her arms in the air, but she settled for a big smile as the judge pinned a yellow ribbon on her mare's sparkly browband.

"Fabulous job," Liz said, as Kate trotted up.

Her ribbon joined the others on the van's windshield. Timber Ridge had moved into second place, just a few points behind Larchwood and fifteen ahead of Spruce Hill Farm.

Next up was gambler's choice.

While Holly and Adam prepared for their class, Kate kept a sharp lookout for the guy in tan jodhpurs. Was it Richard North or just the father of someone in her pleasure class? Holly hadn't even noticed him. Surely, if he was coming to the show, he'd be here by now.

Adam went first. He blistered over the jump course, cutting corners and taking fences from impossible angles. Domino didn't knock a single one down.

"Wow," Holly said, when Adam rejoined them in the collecting ring. "That was awesome, dude." She gave him a fist bump, then gathered up her reins. "But I'm gonna beat you."

Kate held her breath as Magician catapulted through the start gate. He flew over the brush jump, made a tight turn, and cleared the parallel bars with inches to spare.

Holly swung right and in two strides, they leaped over the hogsback.

"She's nuts," Liz said, as Holly whipped around and aimed herself at the in-and-out.

Adam closed his eyes. "I can't watch."

Kate winced. Holly was taking a huge risk, only giving Magician three strides before the tricky double jump. But her magnificent horse cleared them both.

"Phew." Kate exhaled.

Liz said, "She might even win."

Kate glanced at the clock. There were four other clear rounds, including Adam's. But his time would be hard to beat. Holly thundered toward the five-bar gate. Magician hesitated and almost swerved away. Holly checked him in time and they soared over it without a mishap. Only one more fence, and she had it made.

The audience grew quiet as Holly and her black horse approached the red wall. With a gigantic leap, Magician threw himself forward. His hind foot clipped the top row of bricks.

"No," Kate cried. "It's gonna fall."

The brick wobbled. It teetered both ways, but held firm. The audience erupted in a frenzy of clapping as Holly and Magician galloped through the finish line.

"She did it," Liz cried. "She went clear."

"Faster than me," Adam said, grinning.

Moments later, he joined Holly in a victory lap. They rode side-by-side. Adam held his red ribbon in his teeth while Holly waved her blue one at the crowd. Everyone cheered. They probably didn't realize these two gleeful riders were on rival teams. At this point, it just didn't seem to matter ... until Angela rode by, scowling as usual.

Kate gulped. In less than two hours she'd be competing against her worst enemy. Except this time, they really would be on opposite sides.

15

HOLLY'S MAGNIFICENT WIN put Timber Ridge ahead of Larchwood. An hour later, Adam narrowly beat Jennifer in the trail class, and the teams were even again. Their last event—junior jumping—would decide the championship.

Kate spent the next twenty minutes warming up and trying not to freak out. So far, none of the other riders in her class had clear rounds. Angela rode by on Skywalker. A line of neat little braids marched down the crest of his neck; his bay coat shone like a bronze button. Even his bridle gleamed. The Larchwood grooms had polished him to perfection.

"You don't stand a chance, Kate McGregor," Angela said. "Why don't you quit and go home? You'll only make a fool of yourself."

"Like you just did?" Holly said. "By changing sides?"

Ignoring her, Angela cranked up a full-wattage smile and beamed it straight at Adam. "My mother's throwing a big party," she said. "For *our* team. You *are* coming, aren't you?"

"When?" he said.

"Right after we win the championship."

"I'm sorry, Angela," Adam said, sounding not the least bit sorry. "I'll be celebrating with Timber Ridge because Kate's gonna win this class."

"Traitor," Angela snapped.

Holly said, "Takes one to know one."

Adam laughed so hard that he almost fell over. The loudspeaker called Angela's number. She glared at Adam, dug her heels into Skywalker, and cantered off. As Kate watched her go, she caught sight of Liz at the rail. She was talking to the guy in tan jodhpurs. He glanced toward Kate and tipped his baseball cap again.

She wanted to throw up in it.

* * *

As Kate had feared, Angela got a clear round. Skywalker sailed over the tricky course without a single mistake, and they left the ring to a round of applause.

"See, what did I tell you?" Angela said. Her voice

dripped with scorn. She yanked off her helmet and out fell a mane of black hair. "I'm going to win."

Kate's nerve took a nosedive.

The only way she could beat Angela now was to get a clear round as well. Then they'd have to face each other in a timed jump-off. Memories of the Hampshire Classic shot through her mind. She'd allowed Angela to win that one, but she wasn't about to let it happen again.

Two more riders went—neither one of them clear—and then it was Kate's turn. She adjusted her hard hat, gathered up her reins, and risked a quick glance toward Liz. The guy had disappeared. Maybe he was just someone's dad, or perhaps he'd been talking to Liz about boarding a horse or taking lessons at Timber Ridge.

The judge's whistle blew.

For a split second, Kate couldn't remember the course. It was a convoluted figure eight, and if you took jumps in the wrong order, you got eliminated.

Think, Kate, think.

She shook her head, and everything swam back into focus. They weren't jumping against the clock, so Kate took her time. She cantered Tapestry over the brush, then the crossrail, and eased her into a wide circle so they'd have a straight run at the hogsback. Over they went, then came a sharp left turn toward the gate. Tapestry gathered herself up and cleared it with room to spare.

This is fine.

Four jumps done; five more to go.

But as they approached the hay bales, Tapestry faltered. Two horses had skidded to a halt at this yummy jump. They'd wanted to eat it, rather than jump it.

"This is not a snack," Kate warned.

After a moment's hesitation, Tapestry popped over the hay bales with what felt like a sigh of disappointment. Kate bit her lip to keep from laughing out loud. This wasn't the time for giggles. She had to concentrate, hard.

Coming up was the in-and-out, a tricky combination that had caused most of the problems so far. First was a single oxer, followed by a set of parallel bars. One horse had demolished it; two others had refused and been eliminated. Kate swung a hard right.

"One, two, three," she said, as Tapestry took off.

Clunk!

The oxer's top rail wobbled, but it didn't fall.

Kate let out her breath, unaware she'd been holding it. Tapestry's ears flicked back and forth, waiting for Kate's next cue. They had two strides—maybe three—before the parallel bars. Tapestry took only two and soared over the jump like a big golden bird.

"Awesome," Kate said, as they landed.

She made another right turn. Ahead was Tapestry's

nemesis—the chicken coop. Liz had insisted this show never had one before, but this time, it did. Mrs. Dean had probably ordered it special for Kate and made sure it was as scary as possible. Not only was the coop bright orange, it had wooden cutouts of chickens on one side and a scarecrow on the other.

A scarecrow?

Kate gulped. She kept her hands light, her body loose and fluid. If she let Tapestry know for one single second that she was scared to death, her mare would dig in her toes and Kate would go flying over her head.

Tapestry snorted. She skittered left, then right. She tried to turn a circle, but Kate kept her straight. Circling in front of a jump counted as a refusal.

"It's okay, girl," Kate whispered.

Her old riding master once said, *Throw your heart over the fence, and your horse will follow.*

So Kate urged Tapestry forward. She tossed her heart, her brain, and her determination over the coop. Tapestry didn't let her down. She followed Kate's heart right over the jump as if she'd been doing it all her life.

One more to go—the wall.

It loomed like a red menace. On each side were white wings with vertical slats. A white pole rested six inches above the wall; another lay in front of it. Tapestry put in an extra stride and Kate was sure she'd blown it. They were much too close. She should've given Tapestry the signal sooner. They couldn't possibly clear it.

The crowd let out a collective, "Ooohhh."

Leaning forward, Kate felt as if they were climbing a ladder. Tapestry launched herself upward, tucked in her legs, and leaped over the wall like a kangaroo.

They landed with a thud.

"Another clear round, folks," said the announcer.

There were twenty riders to go. It would take another hour, maybe more, before the final jump-off.

*   *   *

Liz was waiting at the trailer. She gave Kate a hug. "That was a fabulous ride," she said, and her face turned serious.

"Mom, what's wrong?" Holly said.

"Brace yourself, Kate," Liz said. "Mr. North's here."

"Where?" Kate said, feeling sick.

Liz pointed to a black truck with New York plates and a four-horse trailer hitched up behind. Its ramp yawned open. "He's pretty sure Tapestry's his horse, but he wants to make absolutely sure."

"How?" Holly said.

Just then, the man in tan jodhpurs led a chestnut mare down the ramp. She had a white star on her forehead, a long flaxen mane, and a silvery tail that streamed behind her like a gossamer flag.

"It's Tapestry's twin," Holly exclaimed.

The man shook his head. "No, it's her mother."

His mare whinnied, then jerked the lead rope from his hands. She rushed up to Tapestry and nuzzled her face. Tapestry nuzzled back. She went into submissive foal behavior, clapping her mouth and tilting her head sideways.

Kate wanted to cry. It was beautiful and sad and awesome, all at once. With tears in her eyes, she looked at Richard North's golden mare. "What's her name?" she said.

"Melody," he said. "She's twenty-five years old, and Serenade was her last foal." There was a pause. "She's had twelve, and she never forgets any of them."

"Serenade?" Holly said.

He pointed to Tapestry. "That was her name."

She was a mirror image of her mother—the same copper-colored coats, blond manes and tails, and white stars. They even had identical comma-shaped chestnuts on the insides of their forelegs.

"All Melody's foals have them," said Richard North.

"I want to buy her," Kate said, looking him in the eye.

He pulled an envelope from his pocket. "And I want to give you this," he said, "for rescuing her."

"I don't want a reward," Kate said, waving it away. "I want my horse."

"Open it," he said. "Please."

She ripped open the envelope. Inside was a check for five thousand dollars, made out to Kate McGregor.

Holly gasped. "Wow!"

Kate felt herself slipping away, losing control. She bit her lip, determined not to cry. She thrust the check at him. He took it but didn't put it back in his pocket.

"I've been watching you all day," he said. "I wanted to see you and Serenade in action. She's not an easy horse, but you've formed a real bond with her. I can't tell you how impressed I am." He paused. "And here's another thing. None of us realized she could jump. We train our Morgans for Western and saddle seat, not jumping."

"How old is she?" Liz said.

"She turned six on March fifteenth."

"That's your birthday," Holly squealed, pumping Kate's arm.

Richard North pressed the crumpled check into Kate's hand. "Take this, please. It's your money," he said. "And if you still want to buy Serenade, the price is five thousand."

It took a moment for it to sink in. "You mean," Kate

said, looking at the check. "If I give this back to you, I get to keep my horse?"

"Yes," he said. "But on one condition."

"What?" Kate said, wiping away her tears.

"That maybe in two or three years you agree to breed her to Maestro, my best stallion, and I get first refusal on the foal." He smiled at her. "It might be good timing for, say, when you go off to college."

"That's more than a fair deal," Liz said.

Richard North gave Kate another envelope. "Her pedigree and registration," he said. "She's a purebred Morgan, and if it wasn't for you, I'd have lost her bloodlines forever. So thank you for rescuing her. I owe you, big time, for this."

The loudspeaker burst into life.

"Sounds like they're ready for the jump-off," Liz said. "Are you sure you're up to it?"

Stunned into silence, all Kate could do was nod. Now that she knew that Tapestry was really hers, she'd jump the bleachers if they wanted her to.

16

THE RING STEWARDS RAISED FENCES and reset the timing clock. The four riders in the jump-off had only five fences this time—the brush, the hogsback, the oxer, the parallel bars, and, finally, the wall. The loudspeaker announced the order of jumping. Kate would go first. She didn't know whether to be relieved or not.

"If you take it carefully and get a clear round, you stand a better chance than if you rush it," Liz warned. "Don't watch the clock. Just concentrate on going clear."

"Good luck," Richard North said. He held up his check, now torn in half. "I'm betting on Tapestry to win."

Kate grinned at him. He'd called her Tapestry, not Serenade. After all this was over, she would ask him if it was possible to change a horse's registered name or if

Tapestry would always be Serenade as far as the Morgan horse registry was concerned.

The bell rang, and Kate forgot about names and registries. All that mattered now was jumping. Tapestry tore through the starting gate and jumped the brush. The moment she landed, Kate pulled a sharp left, giving her only three strides to approach the hogsback. It was an enormous risk. She probably ought to have swung right and gone around the other side of the coop and given herself a better run. But this route was faster.

Tapestry skidded but managed to take off anyway, and Kate held her breath as they scraped over the difficult fence without knocking it down. Kate made another sharp turn and galloped toward the next fence, keeping a sharp eye on the one beyond.

They leaped over the oxer, took two big strides, then cleared the parallel bars. Now just the wall was left, and she had to hustle. The crowd fell silent. All Kate could hear was her heart, thumping in perfect rhythm with her mare's pounding hooves as they flew toward the wall.

Tapestry took off, and Kate leaned forward. It was a magical feeling—soaring upward on her very own horse. She had Tapestry's registration papers tucked in her pocket like a talisman.

The crowd erupted the moment they landed and zoomed through the finish line. She'd gone clear, and a glance at the clock told her she'd done it in forty-five seconds.

"Well done," Liz cried.

Holly and Adam both said, "Epic."

"Wonderful job," said Richard North, holding up his camera. "I've got lots of photos to share with my family. They'll be thrilled about this." He shook Kate's hand, promised to keep in touch, and headed back to his truck.

"Nice guy," Liz said.

The next rider went clear but took fifty seconds to do it. The one after had eight faults, so Kate was still in first place. Then, it was Angela's turn. She galloped like a maniac over the brush, pulled an even tighter turn than Kate's, and cleared the hogsback.

Clods of dirt flew from Skywalker's hooves as he skidded around corners. He flew over the oxer and the parallel bars. The clock showed thirty-five seconds. Kate closed her eyes as Angela raced toward the wall at full tilt.

The crowd gasped.

Kate's eyes shot open, just in time to see Angela and Skywalker demolish the top row of bricks. They galloped between the finish posts at forty-two seconds, but it didn't matter. Kate's clear round had trumped Angela's four faults at the wall.

"You've won," Liz said.

Holly hugged her. "You've finally beaten Angela Dean."

"Yeah," Adam said. "And you guys have nailed the championship."

Whooping with delight, the other girls clustered around Kate and her horse. Jennifer planted a kiss on Tapestry's nose; Sue and Robin thumped Kate's back so hard that she almost fell over. In a daze, Kate wrapped her arms around Tapestry's warm neck.

She'd beaten Angela and helped her team win.

But best of all, *she'd done it on her very own horse.*

Don't miss **Book 5** in the exciting **Timber Ridge Riders** series. Coming in March, 2013

Chasing Dreams

NOW THAT SHE HAS THE HORSE of her dreams, Kate McGregor's next dream is to live in Vermont near her best friend, Holly Chapman. She wants to ride for the Timber Ridge team and attend high school with Holly. But Kate's father has other plans. He wants Kate to sell Tapestry and move 2,000 miles away.

So does Angela Dean.

She will stop at nothing to force Kate and her horse out of Timber Ridge ... even if it means putting herself at risk by cheating and letting Kate take the blame for something that's not her fault.

Then Angela's little sister, Marcia, reveals a big family secret, and everything changes.

About the Author

MAGGIE DANA'S FIRST RIDING LESSON, at the age of five, was less than wonderful. She hated it so much, she didn't try again for another three years. But all it took was the right horse and the right instructor and she was hooked.

After that, Maggie begged for her own pony and was lucky enough to get one. Smoky was a black New Forest pony who loved to eat vanilla pudding and drink tea, and he became her constant companion. Maggie even rode him to school one day and tethered him to the bicycle rack ... but not for long because all the other kids wanted pony rides, much to their teachers' dismay.

Maggie and Smoky competed in Pony Club trials and won several ribbons. But mostly, they had fun—trail riding and hanging out with other horse-crazy girls. At horse camp, Maggie and her teammates spent one night sleeping in the barn, except they didn't get much sleep because the horses snored. The next morning, everyone was tired and cranky, especially when told to jump without stirrups.

Born and raised in England, Maggie now makes her home on the Connecticut shoreline. When not mucking stalls or grooming shaggy ponies, Maggie enjoys spending time with her family and writing the next book in her TIMBER RIDGE RIDERS series.

Made in the USA
Lexington, KY
19 May 2013